One Potato, Tu

BOOKS BY GAYLE PEARSON

Fish Friday

The Coming Home Cafe

One Potato, Tu

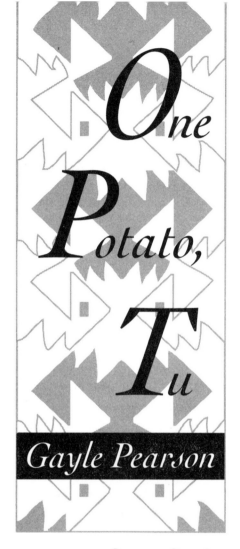

One Potato, Tu

Gayle Pearson

Seven Stories

ATHENEUM 1992 New York
MAXWELL MACMILLAN CANADA Toronto
MAXWELL MACMILLAN INTERNATIONAL
New York Oxford Singapore Sydney

Atheneum
Macmillan Publishing Company
866 Third Avenue
New York, NY 10022

Maxwell Macmillan Canada, Inc.
1200 Eglinton Avenue East
Suite 200
Don Mills, Ontario M3C 3N1

Macmillan Publishing Company is part of the Maxwell
Communication Group of Companies.

FIRST EDITION
Printed in the United States of America
10 9 8 7 6 5 4 3 2 1

Book Design by Black Angus Design Group

Library of Congress Cataloging-in-Publication Data

Pearson, Gayle.
      One potato, Tu/Gayle Pearson. — 1st ed.
         p.   cm.
      Summary: Life is always interesting in twelve-year-
old Lindsey's family, whether her mother is going off to
summer camp to escape the kids or big brother Eric is
being forced into a bird-calling contest by a bet with a
neighbor.
      ISBN 0–689–31706–9
      [1. Family life — Fiction.] I. Title.
      PZ7.P323120n   1992
      [Fic] — dc20   91–22307

For Elizabeth,
Matt,
Mike,
Scott,
Brigette,
and Alyse

ACKNOWLEDGMENTS

The author extends a special thank-you to Linda Adler.

Contents

At Camp Run-a-Muk

*L*indsey was embarrassed to tell other kids the truth, so she sat out back by herself in a strip of shade against the garage. She closed her eyes for a few seconds, sipping a mouthful of lemonade up through a straw. She opened them again just as Jordan Chatworth swept around the side of the house on his bicycle like a boy with a mission. He slammed on the brakes just before plowing into the garage, then hopped off the bicycle to examine the skid mark.

The whole point of sitting in the yard alone was to avoid kids like Jordan. How had he found her?

He carefully picked his way barefoot across the grass, his eyes scouring the ground for dog doo. He was always on the lookout for dog doo. He was just that kind of boy.

"Hi, Lindsey. I heard your mother's going on vacation without you."

She slurped noisily from the straw before raising her head to glower at Jordan. "She's not going on vacation."

"That's not what I heard." His voice was shrill, like a teakettle whistling. He leaned an elbow against the side of the garage and crossed one foot over the other.

Lindsey figured that Jordan was destined to be one of those persistent TV reporters who would someday poke a microphone up into the president's nostrils. "I don't care what you heard. You heard wrong," she said.

"Is she an alkie, going to dry out at one of those places? Neil's mom went to one for a couple of months. So did Mills's brother."

"My mother drinks sun tea. She doesn't need to dry out." She wrapped the straw around her thumb. This kid was impossible. She ought to just go inside and help out with Tu.

"A fat farm then? Is that it?"

"Jordan, what would my mother do at a fat farm? Do you remember what she looks like?"

"Where's she going, then? Why won't you tell me?"

Lindsey shrugged, digging into the cup for a piece of ice. "To camp," she replied.

"*Camp?* Sure. Oh, sure."

"Chill out, Jordan. That's why I never tell you anything." She split the ice in two with her teeth. *Crack, crunch.* Her mom would ask her to stop if she saw her. She would say she was going to ruin her teeth.

"All right. What camp, then?"

"Summer camp. It's summer, isn't it?" She dug another piece of ice from the cup and this time hurled it across the yard toward the trunk of the pine tree towering over the redwood fence.

"Course it's summer. . . ." He bent to scratch a scab on his knobby brown knee. "But . . ."

"It's a camp for mothers only." She might have gone to sit under the pine tree by herself, but her brother Tu had left his farm set strewn across the lawn. She hated stepping barefoot on a plastic chicken or fence post hidden in the grass.

"For *mothers only,*" he repeated, suddenly grinning.

"Jordan." She turned and glared at him. "Try to act normal. Stop shrieking."

"Normal? Look who's talking. What do they do at this *mothers'* camp, have babies and do dishes?" His head bobbed in a silent, yukky sort of laugh, same way his dad, Lawrence, laughed. "Hi-yuuk, hi-yuuk."

"No Jordan, that's not all they do. Besides swimming and crafts they do storytelling and journal writing. They grow herbs and do yoga and have full moon circles."

"Yoga? Can't she stand on her head at home?"

"Stupe. They also go white-water rafting."

"Really? Wow!"

"Plus singing and . . ." She paused, trying to remember what other things her mother had mentioned. "Camp-fires," she added. "Painting, bird-watching . . ."

He looked puzzled and thoughtful. She could imagine what he was thinking. A circle of grown women around a campfire, eating s'mores. It didn't seem natural or right. She could see them all getting ready for bed, swabbing their faces with white gooey night cream that resembled the inside of a well-done marshmallow. She'd wondered about a lot of things — did somebody order them off to bed or did they get to stay up as late as they wanted? If the campers were grown women, then how much older were the camp counselors? Now she could think of a dozen things she'd forgotten to ask, and her mother was inside the house almost packed and ready to go. Lindsey wasn't sitting outside alone only to avoid kids like Jordan. She also didn't want to watch her mother finish packing.

"What's the camp called?" asked Jordan. The sleeves on his T-shirt were rolled up like his dad's always were, only his dad had muscles.

"I don't remember. Something like Wannamucmuc or . . . I don't know."

"Run-a-muk-muk. Hi-yuk, hi-yuk."

"Yeah, Jordan, right." She yawned to show her indifference and stood up, just as her father emerged from the back door waving her in. "I've got to go. See ya."

"*Hey.*"

"*What*, Jordan?"

"Why's she going to camp anyway?"

"Why? *Why?* Because, that's why!" She stamped inside, letting the door bang shut behind her.

Lindsey's mother, Anne, fished around inside her purse for a piece of tissue. The whole family, except for Lindsey's brother Eric, gathered on the front porch to see her off. In khaki shorts and a crisp white T-shirt, Anne was flanked by a duffel bag and backpack on one side and Lindsey's brother Tu on the other. After Tu had arrived from Asia, Lindsey's parents had chosen a western name for him, but somehow he was still called Tu. Right now he was about to swallow his thumb. His nose ran in a steady stream onto his upper lip.

"Blow," said Anne, bending on one knee. "Again." She kissed him, then stood to kiss and hug Lindsey. I'll miss you the whole time," she said. "I'll send you a postcard soon as I get there."

"Okay," Lindsey replied, letting her arms slide from her mother's neck. Her mother smelled good and familiar, like fresh soap and almond shampoo. As a wave of sadness swept through her, Lindsey felt suddenly awkward. She was twelve and did not want to seem like a baby about her mother's leaving. Besides, her mother needed some time to herself. She clasped her hands behind her back and tried to look cheerful and composed.

"Don't forget to floss," said Lindsey's father, Jeff.

"Tell Ellen to take it slow on the roads. Be nice to the other campers, don't swim alone, change your underwear every day, and call if you feel homesick."

"Oh, you," said Anne. She swatted him affectionately on the shoulder and hoisted the backpack up onto her back. "I miss you all already. Don't forget to take your vitamins." She kissed Lindsey's dad on the lips, then picked up the duffel bag and started down the steps as her friend Ellen rounded the corner in a small red convertible.

Tu waved a weak good-bye with his left hand, his right thumb still glued to the inside of his mouth. He nearly smiled as his dad swept him up off his feet and kissed him on his pudgy cheek. "Kiss and hug, kiss and hug, smack your sweetie on the mug," Jeff sang, waltzing around the porch.

Lindsey threw her arm over the railing, shading her eyes with her other hand. It was midmorning and already hot. Camp Run-a-Muk, or whatever it was, was situated near the Tuolemne River. It'd be really hot there, but her mom would get to go white-water rafting. White-water rafting. Didn't people sometimes drown doing that?

"Look at her," said her dad. "She could still be a high schooler, don't you think?"

Lindsey said yes, though it was hard to think of your parents ever in high school. It was hard to think of your mother going to camp. She waved as her mother slapped the trunk shut and slipped into the passenger seat next to Ellen, then felt a sudden urge to run down to the car and tell her not to go rafting, but she made herself stay where she was. Maybe her mom would decide on her own that it was too risky, with three kids waiting for her at home. No, no, she wouldn't. She'd be the first one into the raft.

As the red convertible swerved around the corner onto Ashby and disappeared, Lindsey could still hear Jordan asking: "Why's she going? Why's she going? Why's she going?" Right at this moment, she didn't want to think about it.

Her father sighed, then clapped his hands together in a sudden try for enthusiasm. "How about a pizza tonight, hey?"

Tu removed his thumb from his mouth. "Yes," he said. Then he slipped it back in.

They hung around the front porch for a while, as if hoping Anne would change her mind and come back herself with the pizza.

"Dig in, gang!"

Lindsey, Eric, Tu, and their dad were gathered around an extralarge pizza on the small kitchen table. In fact, there was no room for plates and barely enough for elbows. That suited Eric, who was fifteen, just fine. He didn't need a plate. He just picked up a piece and gnawed and inhaled, gnawed and inhaled until it was gone.

It was early the same evening. Her dad had been cheerful and enthusiastic all day, as though he were leading a bunch of scouts on an outing. It wasn't like him, and he was driving Lindsey crazy.

She loved pizza, but this suddenly looked unappetizing. The tomato and cheese had all swirled together and a little pool of liquid, probably grease, ran off into the ridge around the cardboard.

"Anchovies," said Eric. "You forgot them on my half of the pizza, Dad."

Four short black whiskers straddled his upper lip. It was hard for Lindsey not to lean over and pull one.

"Just open a can of sardines. What's the difference?"

"A big difference. Sardines are not cool, Dad."

Jeff nodded. "Then I guess if you'd been born a fish, you'd be an anchovy." He winked at Tu.

"No. Anchovies are from the Mediterranean and we're not. I'd have to be a salmon. No, no, a steelhead trout."

"A steelhead," Lindsey repeated. "That fits you."

Everyone laughed. That made her feel good. Her mother would've laughed too, if she'd been here. She'd have to remember to tell her: Anchovies, no—steelhead trout—that fits you.

"Yokpmghgoblflanto," said Eric.

What was that fish with really fat cheeks, she wondered? A blowfish?

"Phogunsalmcuffitoast."

She tried not to watch his jaw move, but it was fascinating. It reminded her of the mandible of a grasshopper she'd examined under a microscope in science class. The grasshopper's head had seemed huge compared to the rest of its body, much like her brother's.

"I wonder what she's doing now." Lindsey tried to

start a normal conversation to distract her from watching Eric eat.

"Who?" asked her dad.

"*Mom.*"

Her father smiled. "She's leading a hike up into the mountains by now. Don't worry about her."

"I remember skmgwhen I glmwent to camp."

Eric, whose good manners had evaporated the day he blew out the candles on his fifteenth birthday cake, was talking with his mouth full on purpose. Her mother would not let him act like this. She glanced at her mother's empty chair and sighed. At least she had Tu. She patted his head and smiled down at him, and noticed a little piece of sausage stuck in his nostril.

"I remember too," said Jeff. "You came home from camp with a suitcase full of clean clothes. You stank."

"Yep. I wore the same T-shirt and jeans all week. Gee, camp was great. I remember the time Rudy Mann chased a girl up a tree and then fell out of it. Busted his knee." He laughed with his mouth partly open, nearly losing a mushroom. Lindsey cringed and turned away.

"What's wrong, Tu Tu?" asked Jeff. Big tears welled up in Tu's eyes and began to spill over. Lindsey's father leaned over him, soaking them up with a napkin.

"Rudy's mom fell out the tree, busted her knee," he whimpered.

"Ohh, noo," his father consoled. "Not Rudy's *mom*. Rudy *Mann*. That's his *last* name. See? Besides, your mom isn't going to climb any trees." He tried to laugh in a confident, cheerful way. "Heh, heh, heh."

"Heh, heh," mimicked Eric. "Heh, heh."

Then Tu started in. "Heh, heh. Heh heh heh."

"Heh heh heh," Eric and Tu and her dad said together. Lindsey couldn't help it and joined in. "Heh heh, heh heh, heh heh heh."

"He was on crutches for six weeks," added Eric.

Lindsey stopped laughing. She pulled at a string of cheese with her fork. The crust on this pizza was too thin. She liked doughy things, which was why doughboys had been one of her favorite foods at camp. A doughboy was like pizza crust you wrapped around a stick and cooked over a fire, then filled with peanut butter or jelly. She recalled the last one she'd made. She'd flung it on the ground when the hem of her pants leg had gone up in smoke, then ran yelling in panicky circles around the fire. Afterward, her counselor, Dippy, told her to get a longer stick. Her doughboy was covered with dirt and she couldn't eat it. There wasn't enough dough to make a new one. Lise di Angelo tried to share hers, but it was black and crispy on the outside and raw goo on the inside, most of which remained stuck to the stick anyway. A lot of things happened at camp. A lot of things could go wrong.

After dinner she helped her dad with the dishes, then turned on the television. Tu was playing in his room. Eric had gone to a ball game with his friend Sam. The house was very quiet. She thought about what she normally did on Saturday nights. Sometimes she and Lorry hung out together, but Lorry was away at Lake Tahoe with her family.

"I heard your mother's going on vacation without you," she heard Jordan say again in her mind. Why didn't Lorry's mother go to Camp Run-a-Muk, she wondered? Why just hers? She picked up the *TV Guide* and flipped through it to Saturday night. Boring. She half sighed and half moaned. What was her dad doing tonight anyhow? Where was he?

The sun had slipped below the houses across the street. She wanted to go to the beach this week, or to the lake at Tilden Park. Pretty soon the night would be over and she wouldn't have done anything. This was summer. At Camp Run-a-Muk they'd be gathering wood for a fire. But would anyone know how to build it?

Seeing in her mind the hem of her mother's jeans go up in smoke she leaped off the sofa and headed down the hall to find her father. Before she got to the living room she could hear Jordan screeching, all the way from the front porch.

". . . And Dad got thrown out of the raft and lost his shoe."

Lindsey stopped dead in her tracks.

Jordan's dad, Lawrence, continued the story. "I rode the rocks on my you-know-what till they pulled me in." He boomed a thunderous laugh. "That white water can make a *man* of you!"

"Gee, I hope not," Lindsey heard her dad say dryly. "My *wife's* the one who's rafting."

Sunday wasn't a bad day. Lindsey and her friend Renee and Renee's two brothers played games most of the afternoon. She almost forgot anything was different.

On Monday she checked the mail for a postcard, but of course it was too soon. She mounted some photographs in an album, then walked Tu to his afternoon preschool on College Avenue.

Jordan had done a good job rolling around the neighborhood on his bicycle, spreading the word like Paul Revere about her mother. Edna June Lampson ran over right after lunch to ask if it was true they'd sent their mother to camp, and where could she get an application for hers? Lindsey was very surprised. Then she ran into both the Singer boys on her way to the library, or rather, they almost ran her down wanting to know where to get their mother an application. They also wanted to know if there was a camp for both mothers and fathers. Lindsey got to thinking it was too bad she wasn't able to run off a blank application on a copy machine. She could have sold them for a huge profit.

After lugging a couple of books home from the library, Lindsey retreated to her room with a bag of corn chips and a root beer. She sat on the floor with her back against her bed and laid the books down in front of her—*Mystery of the Hidden Highway* and *Phil the Fungus and Me*. Opening the *Fungus* book to the first page she began to read but couldn't seem to concentrate. She kept thinking about her own camp, Camp Who-Hee-Ha, where she'd spent a wonderful week each of the previous two summers. All the counselors had bird names. Her favorite counselor was "Cuckoo," who taught horseback riding. Cuckoo was young and pretty and could ride a horse frontward and back, like she was born on it. She also didn't mind trying to teach the clumsiest kid, Shelley Porter, how to ride. But Shelley never learned. She was afraid of heights and transferred to origami.

Lindsey loved camp. She wanted to stay another week but couldn't afford it. Only the weird unpopular kids got homesick and wanted to leave early.

She held the book a little closer, really trying to concentrate on what she was reading. Instead she saw the face of her favorite counselor, Cuckoo. She took that as an omen. Her mother would be "cuckoo" for Camp Run-a-Muk. She would just love it. In her khaki shorts and crisp T-shirts she would be a big hit. They would ask her to stay on longer, maybe even as a counselor.

Cuckoo smiled broadly. Lindsey swallowed. Wait a second, she thought! Why would her mother want to be a counselor? The point of her mother's going to camp, she guessed, was *not* to be a counselor.

Lindsey cracked a corn chip in two with her teeth, weighing the possibilities. Surely her mom would miss all of them, wouldn't she? Yes, she would. She would miss them all so much, she would . . . Lindsey sipped her soda. *Why* would her mom miss them? She was with her best friend, Ellen. She was hiking in the mountains, swimming in that gosh darn river, making lanyards and eating doughboys. She did not have to make oatmeal, do the dishes, or pick up socks. Holey moley, she was *free*.

Cuckoo had disappeared. On the left-hand page of her book she saw a vision of her mother eating a s'more and laughing her head off. On the opposite page her mother howled at the moon as the hem of her jeans went up in smoke. Which was it?

A noisy Steller's jay squawked outside her window. "Oh, go away," Lindsey said irritably.

On Tuesday evening Uncle Mo, Aunt Florence, and their dog, Dolores, came to visit while her father worked late on an assignment. They brought their travel videotapes. They were rich and went to places like Seville, Spain. Lindsey loved her Uncle Mo and Aunt Florence, but she would've preferred reading or TV to their fights about which cathedral or ruin or monastery they were seeing. She fell asleep while Aunt Flo was buying fruit in a Singapore market.

On Wednesday her father was grouchy at the dinner table. "I don't have time for anything but work," he complained. "Deadlines, deadlines."

He covered local news for the *Oakland Tribune,* but his real love was sculpting. He was currently at work on a clay figure her mother referred to as Sweet Magnolia because there was a remarkable resemblance between it and Magnolia, the waitress at the Avenue Eatery. He got terribly crabby when he didn't have time for sculpting.

He looked miserable and glum now, holding his chin up with his hand.

Lindsey looked at Eric. Eric looked at Lindsey. There seemed to be a hole in the conversation. It was because her mother would have said something now, maybe something funny about deadlines. Lindsey tried hard to think of something funny, also, but nothing was coming.

"No time for Sweet Magnolia," she blurted. But it didn't sound the same coming from her. It didn't seem funny at all. In fact, the hole in the conversation seemed bigger. Big enough to fall into, which is what she hoped would happen.

"Be careful, young lady," warned Jeff.

She'd suddenly lost her appetite for Stouffer's lasagna and slid sheepishly from the table. The detested "young lady" echoed in her mind as she slouched down the hall-way. The week seemed to be going downhill.

She lay down on her back on her bed just to think, but the pattern of cracks in the ceiling began to resemble the Toulumne River and its tributaries. She grabbed a pillow and covered her face. This was her mother's fifth day at camp. One of the good things about camp was not knowing people so well when you first arrived. Usually you were nice to each other, partly because you wanted the other kids to be nice to you, partly because you didn't know what they were really like at home. You laughed a lot about everything, even things that weren't so funny. Even if somebody did something stupid, you laughed it off.

Maybe you could apply the same principles to home. You could pretend the members of your family were people you just met, and have a real good time.

So later that evening, when Tu painted Sweet Magnolia's fingernails with Real Red finger paint, Lindsey laughed instead of scolding. Then when he spilled some Real Red finger paint on the living room rug, she laughed very hard and extra long, holding her stomach and rolling around on the floor. Then she got sent to her room. Perched on the edge of her bed, she wondered if there were a camp for mothers and daughters together. If not, there ought to be.

Actually, she didn't mind being sent to her room. She liked her room, tucked away at the end of the hall. Right now it seemed a safe place to be. She turned and belly flopped onto her stomach, picked up the *Fungus* book and flipped it open to the bookmark. She'd only read seven pages since Monday, and could hardly remember what it was about. Some kid who finds a sock under his bed covered with mold, and the mold starts to grow a tiny tongue and teeth and itsy bitsy toes and . . .

She inched forward, dropped her head over the side of the bed, and lifted the bedspread. Underneath the bed were dustballs the size of oranges. She once heard someone say that if you could *imagine* something, then its happening was within the realm of possibility. She didn't want to think that that was true because she had a pretty powerful imagination. She didn't like the idea that anything that came into her head, like her mom floating down the river with only one shoe, could be true.

Lindsey sneezed, and sneezed again, then let the bedspread drop back into place. "Oh, it's just your imagination," her parents sometimes said. She decided now that she liked that they said that. Besides, mold with *teeth*?

When she sat up again she noticed a big black smudge on the wall above her bed. How long had *that* been there. Then she glanced around the room with a sinking feeling. The desk and dresser were filled with clutter. Nothing was in its right place. How long had it been like this? She tried to think back to the weeks before. Had she helped her mother at all? She'd come in late a few nights. Her dad spent a lot of time sculpting Magnolia. And Eric, gee. What could you say?

She chewed on a fingernail, her heart beating hard and fast at the sudden thought that the mothers' camp was a hoax! Her mother and Ellen had gone off on their own, where no one could find them! After all, there'd never been a brochure. Worst of all, her own family had driven her mom to it!

Lindsey ran down the hall to the utility room for a sponge mop and went to work on her bedroom floor first. There were no signs of life underneath the bed, just a missing shoe, a *Seventeen* magazine, and an Oreo cookie enshrouded in one of the dustballs. Like a dust sandwich, she thought.

When the floor was clean she dusted the tops of things,

rearranged all her stuff in an orderly way, and picked up the tangled heap of clothing from her closet floor. Then she attacked the living room rug with a wet sponge. Down on her knees, she rubbed and rubbed, like she could rub away what she was thinking, but she couldn't get the stain to completely disappear. Whenever she thought of her mom flying across the Mexican border in the red convertible, she'd tell herself, It's just your imagination, just your imagination. It was Wednesday night, and she went to bed completely exhausted.

When her father returned from work the next day, he apologized for being in a bad mood at the dinner table.

"How about if we all go to a movie?" he suggested.

Lindsey was watching TV. She inched forward across the floor on her elbows like a seal and flipped to another channel. She was not paying much attention to what she was watching because she was waiting for her mother to call. She expected her to call any minute. She just had a feeling. Her mom would say that she'd be gone for at least another week.

Lindsey realized now that she'd had a short lapse of sanity the night before. Her mother was not in Mexico. She really was at Camp Run-a-Muk. But that didn't mean she wanted to come home at the end of the week because she was having too good a time by now. By Wednesday or Thursday you'd made some good friends and you realized the week would be over too soon. By now you were scheming of ways to stay longer. Her mom would call. She was sure.

"You go ahead," she said. "I'll wait for . . . I'll watch Tu."

Her father stood over her, a puzzled look on his face. "You don't want to see a movie?" he asked. Lindsey always wanted to go to a movie.

"No," she said. "I want to watch MTV. But take Eric, please."

After Eric and her dad left, she made Tu a tuna sandwich. She was not hungry. As they settled in front of the TV, she realized she'd watched more television this week than she usually did in a month. Normally she was too busy. But this week she'd stayed close to home. She had to watch Tu more, for one thing. It could be like this next week too.

The phone rang at 6:33 P.M. She checked her watch as Tu ran to answer it. She heard him lift the mouthpiece off the receiver and say hello. She got up off the floor and went to the kitchen to stand beside him. He nodded his head, unable to talk. Big tears had welled up in his eyes.

"Who is it?" she asked. But she knew. Tu handed her the phone.

"Hello," she said.

"Hi, Lindsey." It was her mother.

"Hi, Mom." Her voice cracked. She couldn't help it. "How's camp?"

"Oh, great!" her mother replied. "I've been swimming in the river and rafting and I have a great tan. I've made some new friends and I've got a lot of good stories to tell. How's everything at home?"

"All right." The clock on the wall in front of her was ticking, ticking. Each second could seem like a long, long time. She couldn't think of anything else to say. She waited for her mom to say something.

"Well, Lindsey, is everything all right?"

Her mother sounded a little anxious. Maybe if everything wasn't all right she'd come home right away. Lindsey wondered if she should make up something. She could say her dad had run off with the waitress. Or that Eric had dropped a bag of fertilizer on his foot. "No, everything's fine," she said flatly.

"Well, good. I just wanted to call. You see, this is kind of hard to say. I mean, here I am this grown woman and a mother and everything and I'm having a great time at camp"—she gripped the receiver a little tighter, afraid it would slip from her hand—"but, honey, I'm *homesick*."

Lindsey made herself a tuna sandwich layered with potato chips. Her mother would be home on Saturday as scheduled. Of course she would be back on Saturday. It was her first time away from home alone.

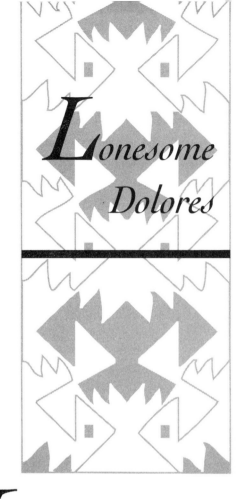

Lonesome Dolores

*L*indsey sat on the eggshell blue sectional sofa next to her Aunt Flo. She rubbed her nose, because sitting near Flo was like being in the perfume department at Macy's. Every so often Lindsey spent the night with Flo and her Uncle Mo, who lived in a big, expensive home in the ritzy Piedmont Hills. It was a treat, because she had her own room with a color TV, just like their dog, Dolores. Dolores also had thick wall-to-wall carpeting and a grooming table, which Lindsey did not have. But that was all right. She did have a telephone and she made the most of an opportunity to call all of her friends from behind a closed door.

In fact, she was spending this particular night at Aunt Flo's and Uncle Mo's because her parents would not permit her to have a phone in her room. She was mad. She came here to get away from them.

Lindsey once asked her mother if Mo and Flo named their dog Dolores because they didn't have children. Her mother pointed out that their neighbors the Ramones had, as well as two children, a dachshund they'd named Pearl, a terrier, Turtle Ann, and two hamsters, Sam and Dave. Two doors down from the Ramones, Gerry and Tom De-Witt were raising Meredith, Mike, Mickie, Olivia, and Josephine, the last two being stray cats that the first three had carried home in a cardboard box one summer. On the other hand, said her mom, look at old Lydia Wells, who played poker most evenings. She had an English sheepdog named Blackjack. In the duplex next door to Lydia, the widower Dalton Fertig kept a parrot he called Luscious. And no one in her right mind would name a kid Luscious or Blackjack.

"He's up to no good," said Flo, under her breath. She narrowed her eyes. Her bosom heaved. It went up and down, up and down very slowly. Lindsey tried to avert her eyes but it was an enormous challenge. She seemed like a wild animal ready to spring.

"I can see it in his eyes. He's restless and up to no

good. He's in one of those moods." Aunt Flo was talking about Lindsey's uncle Mo, standing with his hands behind his back in the arched doorway between the sunken living room and the formal dining room.

Aunt Flo had a favorite line. It was: "If Florence is Flo, why isn't Lawrence Lo?" And she would rattle off the famous Lawrences. Lo of Arabia. Lo Welk. Lo, Kansas. She had to do a little teasing to keep up with Mo. He was a very big tease. He could get Flo really wound up, ready to yank her hair out or his, and Dolores running in circles.

Mo's eyes scanned the living room as though he hoped to get inspiration from the imported Italian coffee table or the original expressionistic paintings covering the walls. He adjusted his horn-rimmed glasses resting on top of his round ruddy cheeks. "I'm bored," he said. "Whattayawannado? Should we play a game or go for a walk or what?"

On hearing the word "walk," Dolores lifted her head and waggled her whole body. Lindsey leaned forward to scratch her fuzzy ear.

Mo, short for Morton, was her father's older brother. Her father said that when Mo was a kid he always said he'd be rich someday. And he was. Her dad said he always knew he wouldn't be. And he wasn't.

Lindsey knew her aunt and uncle had made their money in fancy pizza. They imported the sausage from Sicily and the cheese from France and Norway. They even put fresh flowers in the salads.

Her aunt and uncle didn't seem to work much now.

They traveled and entertained and answered the telephones.

Uncle Mo groaned like a big restless bear and stretched his arms toward the ceiling. Then he lumbered over to the world globe sitting on a wobbly stand on a table against the wall and gave it a spin. "Let's see where it lands," he said with some excitement. He lightly planted the tip of his forefinger on the globe as it spun. "And that's where we'll go on our next trip."

"I knew it," said Flo, her bosom heaving again. "I figured we'd play some stupid game."

Dolores leaped to her feet and began to run in a small circle in the center of the room. Spinning the globe seemed to make her crazy. So did mention of the word "rain." She was a pretty neurotic dog, and not attractive either. Once she'd emerged from Grandpa Don's bedroom wearing his false teeth. When everyone laughed she'd dropped her head and dumped the teeth on the floor. Poor Dolores. Poor Grandpa Don. For ten days after, he'd gone without teeth while they were soaked and resoaked in glasses of soapy water.

Lindsey's mother said that they all could learn from what happened to Dolores. Don't try to be someone you're not. People can spot a fake.

"Bangkok, Warsaw, Madrid," chanted Mo. He rubbed his hand across a large pot belly not unlike the globe he was spinning.

Lindsey smiled and popped a chocolate-covered macadamia nut into her mouth. She got a kick out of Mo. He reminded her of Milly Morris at school. It was because Milly was always up to something too, a character like Mo. Maybe it had something to do with the letter *m*.

She popped another nut into her mouth, glad that she was here and not at home. At home they ate trail mix out of plastic bags. On the good days it was Super Trail Mix with raisins and carob.

"Bangkok, Warsaw, Madrid." The globe still whirled under Mo's pudgy fingertip.

Flo shook her head, her hand tucked underneath her chin. "Tsk," she clucked to Lindsey. "He's just a big kid, isn't he?"

"Flo and Mo, Mo and Flo,

"Wherever it lands is where we'll go."

Dolores was going wild, nipping at the end of her tail with sharp little teeth.

"Hurry up with your game, Mo, before she chomps off her tail. Here, Dolores. Come to mommy. She'll be nice to you." Aunt Flo beckoned with a Mostly Mauve fingernail, which glistened in the afternoon light. Her dress, her eye shadow, even the blush on her cheekbones were various hues of mauve. Lindsey was glad she was not a grown woman yet because she did not want to worry about matching outfits to the color of her skin. Still, she liked to scan the fashion magazines distributed on tables throughout the house.

She reached for another chocolate-covered macadamia nut and buried her bare toes in the thick white carpet. The heavy scent of her aunt's The Lioness perfume was making her dizzy. She got up and crossed the room to see where the tip of Mo's finger would take them, as the globe wheezed to a wobbly stop.

"Hmm," he said, bending to look. "Saugatuck, Michigan." He straightened and gave Lindsey a big smile. "We're going to Saugatuck, Flo. Italy will have to wait."

"Oh, right," said Flo, lifting her chin to gaze out the window behind the sofa. "Saugatuck. Sure."

"Let's see. I wonder what's the best way to get there." Mo scratched his head. "And I wonder if we'll have to worry about—*rain.*"

"Oh, Mo!" said Flo, slapping the sofa. "You're mean."

Dolores slunk from the room with her head hanging down and her tail dipped between her legs. She was heading off to her room, or to a safe spot under someone's bed.

"I don't like it when you tease Dolores like that." Flo smoothed the sofa where she'd hit it. "You make her neurotic."

"Her *is* neurotic," said Mo. He hitched up his pants. "This is fun, isn't it, Lindsey?" He poked her lightly on the arm. "Here, you put your finger down this time. Anywhere you want."

Lindsey looked at her aunt, who shrugged helplessly and picked at a damaged mauve nail. "We used to play bridge, but he got tired of it. I'm thinking of Tonka toys for his birthday."

Mo gave the globe three good spins. Dolores tore back into the room with a crazed look in her eye and took off after her tail again.

"If she ever catches it," said Mo, "she'll find out that you don't always want what you think you want."

"That's real true," said Flo. "After all, look who I married."

"Oh, brother," said Uncle Mo. He shook his head, looking a little peeved. "Don't ever get married, Lindsey. It's never what you think it'll be."

In fact, Lindsey sometimes wondered why they *had* gotten married. They must've at least *liked* each other, but then what happened?

Uncle Mo gave the globe another twirl. Lindsey's arm was getting tired and her finger was hot. She wished she'd filled her pocket full of macadamia nuts and gone for a walk.

"Spin, spin, spin," recited Mo. "Where it lands is where we begin. Dolores, stop that. You're going to have a heart attack." Dolores glanced at Mo briefly, her teeth bared in sort of a mean little smile, but she would not stop.

When the globe stopped Uncle Mo lifted Lindsey's finger and read, "Novokuznetsk, Siberia. Wow. It's going to be hard to pack for Saugatuck and Novokuznetsk both!"

"Very funny," said Flo. "Only I don't feel like laughing."

"Novokuznetsk," Mo repeated, studying the fine black print covering the Soviet Union. "That's good. We can work in day trips to Mongolia and Barnaul, or Minusinsk. Maybe slip down to Prohop'yevsk for an overnight."

"Very funny."

Lindsey thought it *was* funny. "Slip down to Pro-hop'yevsk, ha!" But because of the way her aunt's lips were pursed and her nostrils pinched together, she did not laugh. Aunt Flo's arms were crossed over her chest. Her legs and her feet were crossed too, and Lindsey wondered if that's where the the term "to be cross" came from.

Lindsey shuffled her feet and stared down at the globe. She wanted another chocolate nut but felt awkward about crossing the room in front of her aunt to get one. Should she or shouldn't she? How pathetic. Her uncle had known at age ten that he was going to be rich. Yet she, at age twelve, couldn't decide whether or not to cross the room for a macadamia nut.

She remembered the little pendulum her friend Lorry used to help her make decisions and know the future. She tied a string around a silver ball and held it over a piece of paper on which she'd written four choices: "yes," "no," "don't know," or "maybe." Lorry said you asked yourself a question, like, "Should I wear my purple socks to the dance with Conrad?" Then you held the ball over the paper and your brain sent a signal down through your arm and your hand to the tips of your fingers. The ball would swing toward the right answer.

Dolores stood near the white upright piano, whisking the air with her tail and studying Mo intently, maybe to see how safe she was from the *r* word.

"Here, Dolores, come to daddy," said Mo. He crouched low and rapped his knuckles on the floor. Dolo-res waddled up, eager to forgive him. Mo scratched the white patch on her forehead. "I'm sorry I said the *r* word before." Dolores dropped her head a half-inch and slowed her tail between whisks.

She was a smart dog, if not attractive. She knew what the *r* stood for.

"And I won't say the *r* word again today. Now go tell Aunt Flo to stop being such a crab. Tell her we're only playing." He gave her a slight push in the right direction.

At Lindsey's house, the *r* word meant something entirely different. Her parents used it because they got tired of talking about relationships. So they said things like, "Fritz and Jean are having a tough time with their *r* word right now." She supposed Dolores could have a tough time at her house too. She wouldn't know they were talking about love instead of the weather.

Dolores waddled up to Flo and stood, her long pink tongue drooling onto the floor.

"You just tell Uncle Mo he can go to Novowhatsit by himself and play all he wants. I'll pack his bags!" Aunt Flo recrossed her arms. "G'wan now, Dee Dee." She sometimes called Dolores Dee Dee. "You tell 'im."

Dolores turned and obediently ran back to Mo, her tongue flopping out of the side of her mouth.

"That's fine," said Uncle Mo to Dolores. "Tell her to pack me an extra bag. I'll stop off and see my sister in Waco. Maybe I'll stay for six months. Who knows?" He scratched the soft spot under Dolores's chin. "My sister knows how to treat a guy right. Go tell that to Aunt Florence!"

Dolores covered the distance between Mo and Flo in record time, about a second and a half. But Flo turned her head and wouldn't even look at Dolores. "Don't bother," she huffed at the dog "I'm not listening."

Dolores pivoted, her tongue flinging an arc of drool across Aunt Florence's knees as she sped back to Mo.

Poor Dolores. She was running herself ragged. Lindsey smiled awkwardly. She didn't know if she *should* be smiling so she fixed her mouth in a more neutral position. Life as a grown-up was going to be hard. Lots of little decisions, not to mention the big ones.

"She never listens!" cried Mo. He stood and spun the globe with a quick angry flick of his wrist. It flew off the table and whizzed past Dolores's right ear, like a satellite hurtling through space. Her eyes bugging out of her homely oblong head, Dolores bolted from the room.

The room was suddenly quiet. Nobody spoke. Lindsey didn't know what to do. She *never* knew what to do. She was her father's daughter and would never make money in pizza. The only activity in the room was Aunt Flo's bosom heaving as she glared at the ceiling.

"There, now you've done it," Florence said with finality.

"Lindsey," Mo said solemnly. "Would you be so kind as to re*mind* your aunt who Dolores favors when she's really upset? Who found that tick in Dolores's ear? Who removed the thorn from her paw?" He hitched up his pants with a snap of his wrists and a menacing scowl.

Lindsey looked at her uncle, then stole a glance at her

watch. It was 3:30. She wanted to watch TV. She opened her mouth, "Uh . . ."

"That's okay, Lindsey," said Florence. "Mr. Big Shot is at it again. We'll let him spend his overnight in Mongolia. Maybe they'll listen to him there. Maybe he'll find some poor Mongolian to pick on."

Lindsey studied the floor, shifting her feet. In her mind she saw herself run drooling across the room, from Mo to Flo, then back to Mo. Mo, Flo. Flo, Mo.

"See that, Lindsey? See how she just changed the subject?"

"He knows how much I want to go to Italy. I was named for the town of Florence in Italy. Did you know that, Lindsey?"

Lindsey didn't, and she didn't even have time to shake her head no in reply.

"We've been everywhere *but* Italy. But he doesn't want to go there. That's why he plays this stupid globe game. He thinks he can spin his way out of Italy. He doesn't really *like* Italians and you know what I am? Well, you can guess. I'm not German. I'm not Irish. I'm not . . ."

Lindsey tried to remember if her parents ever talked like this: "He" and "she," "she" and "he."

"See, Lindsey, why Dolores gets crazy?" Mo shook his head and sighed.

Lindsey gazed at the bowl of chocolate-covered macadamia nuts. Her mouth was now too dry to eat one. She shifted her gaze to the window, just as Dolores shuffled across the front lawn.

"It's all my fault," cried Florence.

"Uh . . ." Lindsey tried to interrupt.

"It's *always* my fault!"

"Well . . ." Mo began.

"Uh . . ." Lindsey tried again, "Dolores is outside and I think she's heading across the street."

Flo flew off the sofa with a shriek.

"*Argh*!" said Mo. "*Dolores!*"

"I'll get her," said Lindsey. She pocketed a few nuts on her way out the door. No sign of the dog as she stepped onto the front porch. "*Dolores!*" she called, shielding her eyes from the sun. "Hey, *Dolores!*"

Dogs did not roam this neighborhood freely. They stayed home in their fenced-in yards or went for walks with their owners. Perhaps Dolores jumped out an open bedroom window. Poor Dolores. Lindsey headed down the hill in front of their house. If she were Dolores where would she go?

She looked at the big houses as she scouted the neighborhood. She would love to have a swimming pool and cabana someday. It would be great for parties. If only her dad had been more interested in pizza.

She found Dolores asleep under an evergreen tree next to a stack of firewood. "Dolores," she whispered, then nudged her. Dolores opened one eye, then shut it. It was quiet except for some birds singing. She nudged her again. "Dolores. Flo and Mo will be worried. Aren't you lonesome?" The dog's ear twitched. She covered her nose with her paw.

Lindsey scratched the fur underneath her collar. "I'm sort of running away too, so I know how you feel. You can't stay here, though. You have to come back. We'll watch TV in your room together. All right?" Dolores sniffed with her wet black nose. Maybe that was a maybe. Finally she got up on all fours and followed Lindsey back to her aunt and uncle's.

Lindsey heaved the dog back inside through its open bedroom window. Dolores made a dash for her bed. Then Lindsey went to tell Flo and Mo that their dog was exhausted and resting. They sent in a bowl of vanilla bean ice cream, Dolores's favorite food.

After a little while Lindsey opened Dolores's bedroom door and tiptoed down the hallway into her own room. First she found the yellow spool of dental floss in the bottom of her overnight bag. Then she yanked off a strand and wrapped it around a chocolate-covered macadamia nut. On three sections of a small piece of paper she wrote "yes," "no," and "don't know." Dangling the nut above the paper, she asked herself a question. "Will I ever be rich?"

After several seconds the nut began to swing. It seemed to have a mind of its own, but Lindsey knew it was her mind sending a message through her arm, her hand, and her fingers. The answer was "don't know," which was not much of an answer.

She asked the nut some other questions. "Will I get an *A* in Spanish?" "Will I get the same lunch period as Lorry and Tosh?" "Do I want to have children?" This time she got "yesses" and "nos," so she tried "will I ever be rich?" again. The answer was still "don't know."

She put her homemade pendulum aside and slipped out her bedroom door and down the hallway. Peering around the corner into the living room, she saw Florence and Mo holding hands on the big eggshell blue sofa.

". . . and if Dolores were here, I'd tell her to tell you how much I love you," said Mo.

"I'd tell her to say you're a big palooka," said Flo.

"I'd tell her . . ."

Back in her room Lindsey tried the pendulum again. But this time she asked it a different question: "Do I want to be rich?" The answer was still "don't know," so she untied the nut and ate it. She set the strand of dental floss aside for later. She was really going to need it after all this sugar. Then she picked up the phone and dialed home. She was homesick.

*A*t the Avenue Eatery

*L*indsey scanned the menu at the Avenue Eatery. Every so often her father took her out to dinner alone. They'd been to some good places, like Betty's Ocean View Diner, Soul Brother's Kitchen, and Little Joe's for spaghetti in San Francisco. The Avenue Eatery was the place they came to most often. It was close by and the pies were six inches high in the center.

She readjusted her jacket on the back of her chair so

that the zipper was not digging into her back. Then she picked up the menu again. She might order a burger, fries, a salad, and dessert because she'd had soccer practice and was awfully hungry. Plus, she liked to order red meat when her mother wasn't along. Her mom often said, "If it's red and dead it's not to be fed."

Every time the door opened the wind gusted across the room, making the little yellow flames shiver inside their red candle holders. Lindsey wished it would snow. It seemed cold enough. She remembered it snowing once when she was back in the fifth grade, and school was canceled for the day.

Magnolia, the waitress, flashed them a warm, lingering smile. Then she came by to wipe down the table.

Lindsey's mother called her Sweet Magnolia. She claimed that the clay figure Lindsey's father, Jeff, was sculpting in his workroom looked suspiciously like Magnolia the waitress. Curves and bumps in all the same places — stuff like that. She liked to tease him about it.

"Hi, you two." Sweet Magnolia stood right over them, curves and bumps and all, and she gave Lindsey's father an extrasugary smile and winked.

Jeff blushed when he said, "Hey there, Magnolia," so cool-like back to her. Lindsey knew he'd die if Magnolia found out her name was associated with a slab of clay in his workroom, and how he hammered and chiseled away at all her parts.

"I guess we need another minute," said Jeff. "I think the kid here is still undecided."

"Sure enough, hon." Magnolia slipped the ticket into her uniform pocket and waltzed away to another table.

Lindsey leaned across the table. "Dad, she called you 'hon.' " Her father had on his teal blue sweater and it brought out the blue in his eyes. She understood why a woman would call him "hon."

"Oh," said Jeff, shrugging. "I think she said 'hum.' "

"Hum? You think she said 'Sure enough, *hum*?' Right, Dad." She laughed.

"Well, don't tell your mother. Okay?" He winked at her over the top of his menu.

"Mm mmm."

"No, I mean it. Be sure not to tell your mom."

"Oh, all right."

"No, *really*, no matter *what*, don't tell your mother!" He winked again and grinned.

"Oh, Dad. You're goofy," she laughed.

She didn't always get along with him. He had a strong streak of obstinacy. Last week, for example, they were shopping for ingredients for a mocha bundt cake. He said the recipe called for whole wheat flour only and she said she was sure the recipe said half whole wheat and half unbleached white flour. He bought whole wheat. He was wrong. He made it with all whole wheat anyway. The cake weighed about sixteen tons after baking. Each bite sank to the pit of their stomachs like a large stone. He didn't give up. He said it was delicious and ate it until he was sick.

Sweet Magnolia whizzed by in her very short skirt

with two platters of chicken and french fries. Lindsey wondered how someone got to be a waitress. Was it possible she'd grown up wanting to be one? She supposed not. It looked like a hard job, and boring at the same time. She liked Magnolia and hoped she had someone at home who would wait on her.

Cold sandwiches, hot sandwiches, dinner entrees with salad and potatoes. . . . She cupped her hands over the red candle holder to warm them. Magnolia brought her father some coffee.

"Great. Thanks," he said, and laid down his menu.

Jammed into one of the booths against the wall, a crowd of teenage girls screeched and chattered. Everything seemed hilarious to them. Though Lindsey enjoyed going out with her dad, she couldn't wait to be old enough to do that herself. If I'd gone shopping with Lorry and her mother, Lindsey thought, we might have stopped for pizza. These choices were sometimes hard to make. She would have gone with them if she hadn't gone out with her dad. Her mother hated shopping so they only went when it was absolutely necessary, and by her mother's standards those times were rare. She didn't much like it herself. She'd never be one of the "mall dolls."

Her father was dumping NutraSweet into his coffee. She should bring up something interesting to talk about but it wasn't always so easy. Sometimes you had to give them a topic or they just sat there, dumping NutraSweet into their coffee, and stirring, stirring, stirring. Surely the coffee was all stirred up by now. I mean, it's not *cement*, she said to herself. She wondered if most fathers were like that, say in places like Florida and Alaska, France and China. He could tell a good story on paper, though. She had to admit that. Almost any evening she could pick up the *Tribune* and read a story with his byline.

"So what'll it be, Linny? You won't have to pass a quiz on the menu."

"Very funny, Father." She fingered the menu's tattered edge, suddenly feeling dizzy with hunger. Everyone around them was eating. Ketchup drizzled down a little boy's chin at the next table. His mother twirled pasta around a fork and his baby sister blew an arc of peas across the table.

Lindsey glanced again at the table of girls, where hilarity still reigned. Every single one had her hand on a burger or french fry. "A burger," she said aloud, "and . . ." She was about to say "salad," because she felt the presence of her mother somewhere close to her left shoulder. But she turned to her right and said "fries" instead.

"Burger it is," said Jeff.

At that moment Lindsey spied a solitary figure stuck away at a corner table just off to the right. Her stomach did a little flip-flop. She did not like to see people eating alone. It made her feel sad, blue.

"I wish Magnolia would hurry," she said. "I'm starved."

"Well, I guess she's pretty busy. I'll try to catch her eye, though."

She didn't want to be caught staring, so she raised her

menu a little higher and peered over it at the lone woman. The woman raised the spoon to her lips and blew on it. She put the spoon down and pushed up the sleeves of a heavy dark coat.

"It's a funny way to get someone's attention," said her father, clearing his throat.

"What?"

"To say that you 'catch someone's eye.' You know, like she was just walking by, I stuck out my hand, and bingo!"

Lindsey smiled. "Dad, you have a sick sense of humor."

"Here she comes. Let's be ready so we don't seem like nit-brains."

Lindsey tried to get a better look at the woman alone. Her coat seemed shabby. Her gray hair looked as though it hadn't been combed. Lindsey had a sudden horrible thought, that that could be her mom someday, or her dad. Now she didn't feel hungry at all.

"Maybe I'll just have some tea," she said with a sigh.

"Tea? *Tea?*" Her father looked puzzled and surprised. "I thought you were hungry. What's the matter?"

"I — I was hungry."

"So?"

Lindsey shrugged. "I guess I'm not as hungry as I was. Dad, it just bothers me to see someone eating alone like that." She nodded in the woman's direction.

Jeff turned to look over his shoulder. He scratched the back of his neck and drew his eyebrows together. "Gee, I didn't know she was here. That's Mrs. Glass."

"You know her?"

"Su-u-ure." He sipped from his water glass, taking his time. "I'm surprised to see her here alone. Really surprised."

"Yeah? Why?" She watched the woman break a cracker in two and drop it into her bowl.

"Well, she usually looks like a barnacle, thirty-four grandchildren clinging to her arms and legs. Get the picture? She lives with one of her daughters not far from the lake in a house that's not very big. I doubt she has much privacy."

Lindsey studied her father's face. He knew a lot of people from the newspaper. They were always bumping into someone he'd written about — a pet psychologist, a woman who'd had a lung transplant, a man who'd written a book about the art of flirting. . . .

"I'll bet she doesn't have her own room," continued Jeff. "Bet she shares a bed with one of those grandkids, and the kid's still in diapers and when she wakes up in the morning she's lying on a big wet spot."

Lindsey laughed. "Oh, Father, you don't really know her."

"O-o-oh, yes," he insisted, stretching and yawning. "I don't remember the exact story. Maybe she was the one who won the half-marathon in the senior division last month."

"She doesn't look like a runner to me."

"You've got a point there. I don't remember that coat in the photo. But I wouldn't worry about her, Lindsey, she's getting a well-deserved rest. When she eats at home the kids drool on her spaghetti. Now what's happened to Magnolia? I've got to concentrate on catching that eye."

Lindsey pulled a wisp of hair away from her face and smiled at her father. She knew he loved her a lot and didn't want her to feel bad about anything.

When she looked at the woman alone now she saw an entirely different person, someone enjoying the luxury of time to herself. Her coat was ragged from being pulled on by so many kids. Her hair was messy because she was so busy combing everyone else's. She was only eating a bowl of soup because she loved soup and none of her grandchildren would eat it.

"Bingo," said Jeff.

Magnolia retrieved a pencil and pad from her uniform pocket.

"I'll have turkey on rye, no mustard. Lindsey, you want a burger?"

Lindsey was about to say yes when she noticed the table where the high school girls had been sitting. It was littered with plates smeared with ketchup and bits of food.

"A banana walnut waffle and a cream soda without ice."

"Very creative," said Magnolia. She made a few marks on her pad and hurried away.

Lindsey mused over the fact that her father almost always ordered turkey sandwiches, breaking his routine with tuna or chicken. His tastes were plain. She liked that.

She liked that he wasn't the type of person who wanted to impress people by ordering steaks and fancy wines. She didn't know why she liked that, but she did. She hoped when he finished the sculpture it would make him famous, even if he didn't care about things like that.

". . . starved," her dad was saying, drumming his fingers on the table.

As Lindsey twisted her bracelet around and around her wrist, she spied another person alone, a man sitting at a small table near the center of the room. She had not seen him come in. He was a homely sort of person, with a long thin neck and a small head fringed with gray hair, and she hoped that wasn't why he was eating alone. He picked at a salad, absorbed in a paperback book.

"Here, hons." Magnolia set the two plates down on the table. Lindsey looked at the man and then down at her waffle, piled high with sliced bananas, chopped walnuts, and a dab of whipped cream.

"Empire State Building," said her dad. He scraped excess mayonnaise off a slice of rye bread.

The syrup smelled rich and sweet, but she was not sure she could eat it. "Right," she replied. She broke off a piece of the waffle with her fork and then made a face. She couldn't seem to help it.

"What's wrong, Lindsey?"

She detected just the slightest hint of impatience in his tone of voice. "Hmm? I don't know, dad. Maybe I'm coming down with something. I'm just not that hungry after all." She would try to eat, she knew she'd be hungry later on if she didn't, but her stomach had lurched once again at the sight of the old man alone.

Her father studied her for a moment. Then he said, "Well, perhaps you should've ordered something easier on the stomach, soup or some salad, like Art over there." He nodded in the homely man's direction.

Lindsey sighed. She sliced a piece of banana in half and ate it, then a small bite of waffle. She did not look over at the man. "Art?" she repeated. "Don't tell me you know him too?"

"Well, I don't really know him. But someone that I know knows him. She was just saying that she'd heard that Art's wife was out of town visiting relatives and he'd been pretty lonely."

"Oh," said Lindsey. So she was right this time. She kept her head down and tried to focus on her food.

Her dad hurried on. "So my friend said that Art's wife just called him, yesterday I think, just to tell him how much she missed him, and that she was coming home a few days early. I bet that he was so happy he decided to take himself out to dinner, and he looks like he's really enjoying it, doesn't he?"

Lindsey gave in to her curiosity and lifted her head. Art turned a page, sipping coffee or tea. She supposed you could be happy in a quiet sort of way, even if you were alone. You didn't have to be jumping up and down or near delirious with laughter, like the crowd of girls, to be happy.

"Think you can handle that waffle or what?" asked her dad.

"Oh, I'm doing all right," she said. "It's good. Want some?"

The wind battered a cold sheet of rain into their faces as they emerged from the Avenue Eatery. They hurried huddled together down Telegraph Avenue, passing an old woman crouched in an alcove, half buried under a pile of filthy rags. A gray kitten slept curled on her lap. Lindsey gaped at the woman as they passed and then turned her face up to her father's.

"Dad . . ." she said.

He clutched her hand and squeezed it, but he didn't say a word.

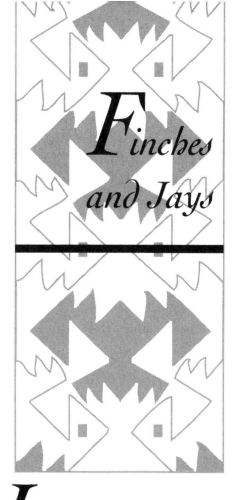

*F*inches
and Jays

I just don't think you have the guts to do it. I'm willing to bet you a hundred on it." Eric's neighbor, Lawrence Chatworth, stood with his feet apart at the bottom of Eric's front steps. His legs in his tight black jeans reminded Eric of two Easter hams.

"I'm not afraid," said Eric. "I just don't want to take the time." He was sitting on the top step, squinting into the sun.

"Sure." Lawrence smiled broadly, showing a row of white even teeth. "C'mon, Eric. Let's see what you're made of."

When Eric was eleven Lawrence bet him eleven dollars that he couldn't eat eleven hot dogs. He'd gotten sick on number eight. When he was thirteen Lawrence bet him thirteen dollars that he didn't have the guts to bring a rose to his teacher on Valentine's Day. He really wanted the money so he brought Ms. Capra a rose. She cried. She'd just broken up with her boyfriend, and had to go home for the day.

Eric's father, Jeff, sitting beside him, chuckled as he peeled a banana. "Careful with your money, Lawrence. He's more a gambler than me, I'm afraid to say."

Lawrence grinned. He shoved his hands into his back pockets. He had a habit of needling Eric. Eric wasn't sure why he got under his skin so fast. He could make him feel like a failure for playing shortstop on the varsity baseball team instead of being a hard-hitting brute on the football team, like Lawrence had been.

Eric could be a brute if he *chose* to be a brute. He looked at his dad neatly peeling back the banana an inch at a time. It just didn't seem to run in the family.

But what was Lawrence up to now? One hundred dollars was a lot of money, but of course he wouldn't do it.

Lawrence crossed his arms, his biceps swelling under his short-sleeved knit shirt. His son Jordan stood nearby, one foot on the ground and one on the pedal of his bicycle. Poor runty Jordan.

"One-fifty," said Eric. He set his gaze on Lawrence's face, seeing in it a flicker of surprise.

Lawrence threw his head back and laughed. "Ho, an opportunist." He began to rock back and forth on his heels, stalling for time.

"Eric." His father glanced at his watch. "Don't forget practice."

"I won't." He shrugged, then began to crack each knuckle on his left hand. He was holding his breath, hoping Lawrence wouldn't call his bluff.

"You could practice for the contest out there at shortstop, in between plays. Kill two birds with one stone. Hyuk, hyuk."

Let the old geezer laugh. He sounded like an old crow. Please, God, don't let me sound like that when I'm his age. Eric looked down at his own legs. He could see some new definition of muscle in his thighs and calves. Then he glanced at Lawrence's ham hocks and scowled.

"Eric." His dad laid the banana peel in a neat pile at his feet. His knobby knees protruded from his khaki shorts.

"I know. Sam's coming by to get me."

"Hundred fifty if you *win*," said Lawrence. "A hundred just to enter. C'mon, Eric. Show your stuff. I'd do it if I were you."

"That's easy to say."

"Oh, *man*. One hundred fifty, then. Three fifty-dollar bills. You got me." He stuck out his hand.

Eric looked at Lawrence's hand in amazement, wishing

it would disappear. When it didn't he grasped it and shook it, trying not to wince from the pressure of his grip. "I got *him*?" He was baffled. How had it happened?

"There you go, buddy! Now we're talking!"

He shrugged like the whole thing didn't mean much, a bet for one hundred fifty dollars that put him in his high school's *birdcalling* contest. He was out of his mind. Except that down deep he knew he'd never do it. He had no intention of going through with it, nor of losing the money. He'd get out of the silly bet somehow.

He glanced at his dad, who rolled his eyes and laughed weakly. Eric was grateful he had not intervened.

"Hah!" said Jordan, shoving off the pavement with his left foot. "Eric's gonna lose a bet with my dad. Hiyuuk, hiyuuk!"

If Lawrence weren't standing there, Eric would have shoved the runt to the ground and pounded him.

"Well, there you have it," said Lawrence. "All in good fun, right? I don't see how I can lose, though. Hiyuuk."

"We'll see," said Eric. He tried to seem at ease, but found himself clenching his jaw as Lawrence strode backward down the front walk grinning, his chest expanded like a big rooster's.

"I'll be going home to watch the tube now," said Lawrence. "But you'd better get busy. Now you've got to practice balls and *calls*. Hiyuuk." Jordan took off after him, cawing like a crow.

"Eric." His dad picked up the banana peel with two

fingers and rose to his feet. "Are you really going to do this?"

"Aw heck, Dad, I don't know. He's just so *macho*." He looked down, focusing on the muscles in his thighs, flexing and releasing. "He thinks he's such a *dude*."

When Eric returned from school the next afternoon, Jordan was riding circles around the fire hydrant in front of his house, jumping his bike up over the curb again and again. It bugged him.

"You're going to ruin your tires, Jordan. It's not a trail bike, you know."

"Two to one says I don't," he squealed. "Bet you a dollar."

"No thanks. Nice shirt, Jordan." Whistling, he took a left turn up the sidewalk toward his front steps.

Jordan looked down at his shirt, which said JUST VIS-ITING THIS PLANET. Then he slowed to a stop and pulled a smashed-up-looking Milky Way from his pocket. "C'mon, a dollar. You chicken or what?"

"Nope. I guess I just don't care about your bicycle. See ya."

"Bet you a buck I can ride no-handed."

"Have fun, Jordan. Don't break your neck."

Right now, anyone connected to Lawrence he could do without. That stupid bet was on his mind the whole day. He did not want to be in the birdcalling contest. He did not even want Lawrence's money, but he could not simply say he'd changed his mind. Maybe Lawrence would just forget about it. He threw his gym bag on the closet floor, a poof of dust enveloping his shoes.

He crossed the room, flinging off his Nikes, and flopped onto his bed. He could just imagine the kind of kids who did this bird thing. After all, bird rhymed with nerd. They'd be captains of the chess club, or class clowns like Dru Showalter who made the most of every opportunity to look foolish. Some kids grabbed the stage any chance they got. He never understood it. He did not want to be singled out, unless he made a nice put-out or drove in a run.

He removed his filthy gray socks and flung them on the floor. He ought to do some geometry before dinner, so he wouldn't have to spend the whole night on homework.

It was a warm February afternoon with a strong hint of spring. Sunlight poured through the open window. The birds were chirping like crazy, "Cree cree cree." He yawned, drowsily scanning the room. His gaze came to rest on his bookcase, the bottom shelf illuminated in a shaft of yellow light. It contained the books he never read: his old *Boy Scout Handbook, Mary Poppins, The Field Guide to Western Birds*.

He yawned again, cracking his jaw, stretching his legs out to the end of the bed.

"Cree cree cree."

"Cree cree cree," he repeated, suddenly laughing about the whole thing with Lawrence.

"Cree creee creeee *creee creeee* . . ."

"All right, I heard you."

"Creee creee cree creeeee creeee!"

The bird sounded ready for attack. Eric sat up and leaned toward the window. It was Jordan, standing in the bushes. He slammed the window shut. *"Creep,"* he yelled silently. *"Birdbrain!"* Then he lay back down and fell instantly asleep.

The first thing he remembered on waking was something that happened to him when he was about six years old. He was at summer day camp. On the first day the counselor divided the kids into groups: sparrows, finches, bluebirds, and jays. He was a finch, but he wanted to be a jay. Finch rhymed with pinch and reminded him of Aunt Debra squeezing his cheeks. The jays sounded like a baseball team. You wouldn't call a team the finches. How would that sound? The New York Finches? The St. Louis Finches? Finches were small, delicate, sweet. He didn't want to be that. Jays were big, meaty squawkers.

The next day the counselor said, "Sparrows and finches over here! Sparrows and finches on this side!" He tried to slide over to the jay side but she caught him.

"You're a finch, aren't you?" she said. He lied and told her he was a jay. But his conscience kept him awake half the night. The next morning he admitted he was a finch. The counselor gave him a pat on the back and he got to be the captain of the finches. The jays had an easy time coming up with a slogan. It was Hey, Hey, Jays. Theirs was Inch by Inch Finches. He still remembered that.

He decided that the next time he saw Lawrence he

would mention the bet as though it had been a joke. Really make light of it. That should get him out of it—a difference of interpretation. He curled his toes and sighed with relief.

The next afternoon he washed the car about the time he thought he might see Lawrence returning from work. He did. Lawrence waved from across the street, his sport coat slung over his shoulder, his gold earring glinting in the sun. He didn't have the guts to approach him. Solemnly he finished the car. He'd have to think of something else akin to getting sick on the eighth hot dog.

He held the book away from his face and shook it, so as not to breathe in the dust. He sneezed anyway, a big, loud "Achooo!"

His younger sister, Lindsey, appeared in his doorway. "I heard about the contest. Are you practicing?"

"No, I wasn't *practicing*. Jeez, I just sneezed."

"Well, you sounded like a whooping crane. What are you reading?" She seemed surprised to see him with a book in his hand.

He shrugged and tossed the book on his bed. "I'm not reading anything. Don't you have some homework?"

"All caught up. You could get tapes out of the library, you know. I mean with bird calls. I've seen them. They're not in the rock section, though. You'll have to hunt for them or ask the librarian. Did you tell Sam about this? I've got stuff to do." She disappeared without waiting for an answer.

He'd lifted the *Field Guide to Western Birds* from his

bookcase just out of curiosity. Some of the pages were stuck together and stained brown. He flipped quickly through the pages of woodpeckers, doves, nuthatches, mockingbirds, geese, gulls, and sandpipers. "Common loon," he stopped to read. "In flight, downward droop of neck and feet gives a sagging look. . . ." That was a bird he could understand. He went on reading.

"Voice: On breeding waters, a long falsetto wail, weird yodeling, maniacal laughter . . . flight call a short, barking *kwuk*."

What was a barking "kwuk?" "Kwuk," he said under his breath. "Kwuk." He got up and closed the door. He tried it again standing up with the book in his hands, and then a barely audible "yodel-lee-eeee-oooo." Even in the privacy of his own room, he blushed. Shoot. He threw down the book and rushed out of his room, out of the house, and across the street to the Chatworths'. He took the steps two at a time and stood on the landing with his hand raised, ready to knock. He could see Lawrence coming down the hallway. He spun around and flew down the steps, then jogged all the way to his school and back. Had Lawrence seen him?

He slipped into the activities office at 3:20 P.M. on February 25, the last day to sign up as a participant. He figured he had to do that as a backup, in the slim chance that he couldn't think of a way out of it.

A little bell tinkled as the door closed behind him. The girl behind the desk was a junior. He didn't really know her. She was reading. On the desk was a clipboard entitled "Seventeenth of March Annual Birdcalling Contest and Brouhaha." There were two or three pages of names, but he didn't want to stop to read them in front of this girl. As it was, his hand shook when he wrote his own name.

He picked up his pack, eager to slip unnoticed back into the hallway.

"Hey, wait a second." She glanced up from her book to hand him another clipboard. "You have to list your birds."

"What?" He turned, feeling the color flare in his cheeks.

"You have to list your *main birdcall*, plus two others."

"Oh." The room suddenly seemed warm and he began to sweat. Main birdcall, he thought. "I . . ." he began hoarsely. He cleared his throat, shuffling a few feet toward the desk. The girl was watching him now and his mind seemed stunned, frozen in a stop-action sports shot of a very good play or a very bad one, and this was not a good one. She was staring up at him with these big brown eyes like he was some sort of mutation.

He felt like a stupid ninth-grader. Worse than that. He could see the bird book and all the pages with all the birds, pictures of birds, yes, yes, ones he'd never heard of before, but what were their names? All he could think of were blue jay and robin but he couldn't say those. They were too easy.

He could only think of one bird. He wiped his nose

with the back of his hand. "I don't know. I guess the loon, then."

She tried to cover her mouth with her hand, but he could see the corners twitching in amusement. "Here, you have to write it down." She pushed the clipboard toward him with one hand, barely holding back hysteria with the other.

Lawrence, Lawrence, you big stupid jerk. Tomorrow I'll go . . .

"*Loon.* That's funny." She'd regained control, picked up a book and was skimming the index. "Any particular loon?" She brushed a hand through short light brown hair.

His ears felt like red banners standing out from his head. "No."

"Just a common loon, then?" The end of her sentence exploded in laughter.

He smiled to hide his death wish and nodded.

"Awwrighty. You need two more, though."

He thought he was going to pass out, and began to back out of the room. "I'll bring them by tomorrow."

"How about if we just put something down, anything, and then you can change it later? Here, pick two."

He shuffled toward her, took the book, and read off the first two names that he saw. "Owl, great gray. Owl, great horned." Had he said that out loud? Yes, he had. She was blushing.

But she recovered very quickly. "Loon, goon, croon."

Her nose twitched, turning a blotchy red and white. "This should be fun. Last year I had a bad cold and missed the whole thing."

"Mmm . . ."

"But I'll be there this year." She folded her arms and sat back, as if waiting for him to do something right then.

"I . . . uh . . . I've got to get to practice. . . ."

She cocked her head to one side and then the other, like a nervous little canary, as he backed out of the room. When he was out in the hall again, he turned and dashed toward the locker room. Loon, goon, loon, goon, loon, goon . . . that's what *he* was. This was it. He'd had enough. Tomorrow he'd go tell Lawrence the bet was off and come back here to take his name off the list.

He loved the way the ball went *plop* when it landed in his glove, or snapped into it if it were hit hard enough. He loved the feeling of fluidity in his body as he charged the ball, scooped it up, and whirled to throw. It required intense concentration. The rest of his life fell away. Charge the ball, scoop it up, whirl and throw, over and over.

It was a short but difficult practice and when they were done he asked his friend Sam to drop him off at the entrance to Redwood Park. Sam wanted to play a little "b-ball." Eric said no, he wanted to go for a run. Sam said it sounded boring.

"Yeah," Eric shrugged. "Well . . ." He didn't want Sam to come along. He wanted to run alone.

He started off on a slow jog down a fire trail, holding

himself back. Another runner passed him. He met two women walking a dog and grunted a "hi" as they went by him. They were nice-looking. He wondered what they thought of him. He glanced down at his legs. They looked hard and hairy. Hairier than last year, anyway, and not as thin. They looked good. He liked his legs. They just needed some color, which he'd get soon because warmer weather was right around the corner. The rest of February, then March. He swallowed.

He wanted to run alone because he wanted to think about the girl behind the counter. He didn't know that was why he wanted to run alone, but now that he was doing it he knew it to be true. That is, he both wanted to forget about her *and* to think about her. He wanted to think about her, but he wanted to forget about what happened. He wanted to remember her eyes when she smiled, how soft her hair looked. He wanted desperately to forget how he had behaved. His stomach lurched.

Loon, goon.

Loon, goon.

Loon, goon rang through his mind as each step pounded the hard dirt path.

He'd give anything to rewind the clock back to 3:00 P.M., but since he could not, he made some changes in the scene in his mind that he replayed over and over. He changed the reason he went into the office in the first place. It was to say he had to pay a fine for losing his baseball cap and then she'd asked him what position he played and he said shortstop and she asked him when the first home game was and he told her and she came and he hit three for four . . .

He stopped in the middle of the trail, standing with his hands on his hips gasping for air. When he caught his breath, he noticed it was dead quiet. Not even the leaves were rustling, and the light was fading above the hills and all around him.

He leaned against a gnarled old manzanita tree with one hand, then realized that the tree's solid muscular bulk reminded him of Lawrence, and removed his hand.

"Keeaww keeawww . . . chee chee chee . . ." Dead silence except for the birds. He listened. "Keee keee . . . keeaww keeawww . . ." The longer he stood not moving or making a sound the more they began to sing, until the chorus grew and swelled all around him, a big happy choir serenading his thoughts of the brown-eyed girl behind the counter.

He sat cross-legged on his bed later that evening running his finger down the index of the bird book on his lap. Alder flycatcher, ash-throated flycatcher, beardless fly-catcher. . . . Forget that one! He unconsciously felt for the four dark hairs above his upper lip. Yes, they were still there.

His finger stopped again under the black petrel, which sounded like something caught in an oil slick. He looked it up anyway. Forget that one too. It's call was a "puck-apoo puck-puck-a-poo." He skipped back to the index.

The surf scoter had a nice athletic sound, but the book

said it was usually silent. That would be one way to fool Lawrence, wouldn't it? Next the red-tailed Hawk. That'd be okay. Their best pitcher's nickname was Hawk. But the bird's call was an asthmatic squeal. Man, oh *man*. He sighed, shaking his head. Then he put the book down, tore off his T-shirt, used it to mop the perspiration from under his arms, and tossed the balled-up shirt into the wastepaper basket beside his desk. Swish. He didn't need to prove anything to Lawrence!

No, but he did want to prove something to *her*. He wanted to find a bird that sounded both athletic and smart, one that bore no resemblance to a loon.

Ou was a Hawaiian bird. "Female lacks yellow head," he read. He was shocked. How could *that* be? How could she not have a head? He read it again. "Female lacks *yellow* head." Oh. Whew.

But here was one. "Ferruginous rough-legged hawk." He flipped to the part of the book about hawks. This bird had a "kree-a" or gave a harsh-sounding "kaah" and he thought he could do that, *if* he really went through with this thing, which he still thought was unlikely. He slipped a tape into his boom box and flipped it on as camouflage. Then he tried a couple of "kree-as" and "kaahs," but it was hard to tell what he sounded like because they mingled with and got lost in the "oh-babys" and "shouldn'ta-hurt-mes" and "lost-without-yous" of Chip and the Floppy Disks.

He picked up the book. He scratched his head. He picked at a scab on his knee. He could be a marbled godwit, a herring gull, a semipalmated plover, or a killdeer. There were thousands to choose from. He only needed three. Then, further on down the list, nestled among the geese and grosbeaks, he found his main bird.

At one o'clock the next afternoon Eric returned to the activities office wearing his favorite shirt and best-fitting khaki pants. The bell tinkled again as the door closed. He cleared his throat. What should he say? Finally she glanced up from her book. He blushed as he had the day before, in spite of the little talk he'd given himself outside the door.

"Oh, it's Loon," she said, looking amused again. So far, this was an instant replay.

"Yep," he replied, smiling along with her. "That's me." He figured it was best not to let her know how embarrassed he'd been. Make it seem like he had a good sense of humor, not a bad memory. He was not going to stammer this time either.

"I—I," he began. Clear the throat. Begin again. "I've got the other names." He removed a slip of paper from the back pocket of his pants.

"Wellp," she said briskly, tapping the end of the pencil on the desk. "I reread the rules and guess what? No changes."

"Huh?" He noticed that she wore a little gold hoop in each ear. Her ears were little and shiny, like porcelain.

"But I'll tell you what. We can make a deal. You just do one little loon for me now and I'll let you make any changes you want." She stopped tapping the pencil and gave him a satisfying grin.

One little loon? She was kidding.

"Ha ha." He glanced down at the paper and then up at her face.

"Any time you're ready."

Now his heart began to race. "I don't know the loon, so I can't. I haven't memorized or practiced anything yet. I'm just starting out. . . ."

"This'll be good experience for you. It's just me here, so you don't have to worry."

Sweat began to trickle down the small of his back, and down his legs. It gathered around the band of his jockey shorts. He licked little beads of it off his upper lip.

"C'mon, Loon. You want to be in this, don't you?" She cupped her chin in the palm of her hand.

"Not really. You see, this neighbor . . ."

She made a point of looking at her watch. "Gee, I'm going to have to get going. You'll be doing just one bird then, the loon?"

"*No!* I've—I've got three others. You—you said . . . all right, all right, I'll do it." *Bam bam* went his heart in his chest. The loon, the loon . . . what did it, what did it do? . . . Weird yodeling, that was it, and, and maniacal laughter . . . *bam bam*! . . . How could he *do* that in front of her? . . . In his head first . . . yooo-di-le-iii . . . No! No! He wiped his sleeve across his forehead.

"Ha ha," he tried.

"What?"

"That's what it does. It laughs." He shrugged his shoulders.

She shook her head. "I've never, ever heard a bird do that. C'mon, Loon, put something into it." She glanced at her watch.

Bam bam! This was a heart attack! He squeezed his eyes shut and bit his lip. "Haaaaaa . . . aaah haaaa haaaa!" If only he, Loon, could evaporate. "Ha ha ha hahahahaha hehehe *heheh heeee*. . . ."

His voice broke. He fought to catch his breath, to stifle what nearly sounded like a sob. . . . He hung his miserable, self-conscious head. Click, click went the clock in the room. A student shuffled by outside the door. This was the end of his life. He could hear his own raspy breathing.

"That was really good," she said softly.

He pretended to rub his eye, and wiped a tear from the corner. In his next life he'd be a wise guy. He'd do it and laugh his head off. He'd do it as a rap song. He'd do it, kiss the girl on the mouth, and stalk out of the room.

"Maybe you should keep that bird."

He shook his head. "I don't think I will." He uncrumpled the wad of paper. It was more like a spitball now. The ink had come off in his hands.

She pushed the clipboard toward him. He bent and tried to steady his shaking hand.

"You've been a good sport, Loon. Really. I guess I didn't think you'd do it. I just wanted to tease you."

He tried to make his mouth smile. It grimaced. He didn't want to look at her, but he couldn't help it. She met his gaze and smiled. It was almost an apologetic smile. The lump in his throat would not go down.

The bell on the door dinged. Shoot, it was Sam, ducking his head inside.

"Hey, Eric."

"Hey, Sam."

"Whatcha doin?"

"Oh, nothin'."

"Mm hmm." Sam winked. "Hi," he said to the girl. "Eric's my buddy. He's a great guy. You ought to get to know him better."

"*Bye*, Sam."

"See you on the field."

"Right." If only he, Loon, could fly out the open window.

"You look sick. You all right?"

"Yeah, I'm all *right*. See you out there."

"Are you sure?" Sam cast the girl a concerned look. "He has a rare disease."

She opened her mouth in surprise.

"He's kidding," said Eric.

Sam winked and withdrew his head. Eric hurried to finish his list. Ferruginous rough-legged hawk. Yes, he'd sure scared this girl. He wondered if she'd read his main bird after he left, and laugh at him one more time.

"Guys are funny. The way you show that you like each other."

He finished writing and stuffed the paper back into his pocket. "Yeah?"

" 'Hey, Eric.' 'Hey, Sam.' "

"Um . . . what would you say?"

" 'Hi, Eric.' 'Hi, Sam.' See what I mean?"

"I guess." He had a funny feeling in his chest when she said his name. It was like the bell on the door going *brrrnng*! A big *brrrnng*! in his chest and a little *brrrnng*! in his stomach. He wanted to hear her say it again. "I'm not sure I get it."

" 'Hey, Eric.' 'Hi, Eric.' 'Hey, Sam.' 'Hi, Sam.' "

He did not like to hear her say Sam's name, but he knew what she was getting at. Like Hey, Hey, Jays. He had a sudden desire to tell her that story.

"You don't seem that enthused about this contest."

"I'm not. It's a bet. I can't get out of it."

"Did that Sam dare you?"

"No, not Sam." Did she like Sam? Why did she keep saying his name? "It's this neighbor."

When she handed him a contest information sheet one of her fingers accidentally brushed against his. *Brrrnng!* He felt a sudden intake of breath.

"See you, Loon."

"I forgot your name." A roundabout way of asking her name.

"It's Krista."

"Well, bye, Krista."

"See you March seventeenth." She smiled, and winked.

He was able to smile back. Then, as he pushed his way

through a throng of kids in the hallway, he could not stop smiling.

Eric hired a senior, Anthony Palermo, the Frank Sinatra of birdcalling, for two half-hour sessions a week. Anthony put him on a special diet. He said you wanted saliva but not a lot of mucus, so he suggested restricting his consumption of mucus-producing foods. Eric took it a step further. He found out what his main bird ate and carried a sack of sunflower seeds wherever he went.

He knew that hiring Anthony was an admission of defeat. He could not find a way out of the contest without losing face. He might lose a lot more by entering, but he hoped Anthony would help him avoid being the "worst of show." He also considered dressing in full plumage, but he expected his name would be called anyway.

They practiced in an empty chemistry lab during lunch. It was humiliating at first to have Anthony try to mold his mouth and lips into the right position. Sometimes he could feel Lawrence hovering in a corner, laughing, laughing. He could feel *her* watching too, tapping her pencil as he struggled to learn.

"Make your mouth go like this," said Anthony. "Pretend its your glove and you're about to catch a fly ball." That reminded Eric of that old saying about somebody "catching flies" when he fell asleep with his mouth open. He knew what Anthony was trying to do, but it just didn't work for him, not even when Anthony said that knowing more than one birdcall was like a pitcher's knowing how to throw a fastball, a curve, and a slider. This was not baseball. He did not stand in the infield with his lips pursed.

Sometimes he practiced in the shower. Other times he went for walks by himself in the woods. He'd practice, stop, and listen, practice, stop, and listen. Anthony said the key was repetition. So he usually fell asleep listening to *Common Birds of the Far West and Hawaii*. It was one thing to read about the chestnut-sided warbler in a book, and another thing to actually hear it go "see see see see see Miss Beech'er."

Meanwhile, Jordan really was bugging him, trying to get him to make bets about everything.

"Bet you can't walk on your hands to the end of the sidewalk."

"Two to one says I can untie and tie my shoelaces faster 'n you."

"Bet you can't throw this ball past the street sign."

He tried ignoring him, but Jordan was always hanging around his front porch, riding around and around in circles like a hamster in a cage.

He was on his way out with Sam one night and there was Jordan, riding up and down the sidewalk, Twinkie smudged in the corners of his mouth.

"Hey! Bet you can't tell what bird this is. Coo-cooo-coooo. Hiyuuk, hiyuuk."

Eric strode right up to him. He wasn't in a good mood. His nerves already were shot and he wasn't sleeping too well. He grabbed a handful of Jordan's shirt and he was going to shake him good and hard. "Listen, Jordan!" He looked at Jordan's frightened face and let go. "Bet you a dollar, two to one odds, you can't guess how many pancakes I had for breakfast."

Jordan looked up at him, caught somewhere between scared and surprised. "Pancakes?"

"Hurry up, Jordan. I've got to go."

"Eight!" he blurted.

"*Eight?* You think I'm a *pig*? I had six. Tomorrow you come over with two bucks, okay, or I'll tell your dad."

"Okay, okay," said Jordan, his eyes big as two silver dollar pancakes.

"Weird kid," said Sam as they headed for his scooter.

"Yeah, well, his dad is weird too. Bet me one hundred fifty dollars I wouldn't enter that birdcalling contest at school."

"He did? That is a weird thing to do. Money would've been great, though."

"Will be nice. I'm doing it."

"Sure, Eric, right. And I'm a starting pitcher for the A's this year."

"No, Sam, really." He slid onto the backseat and sighed. "Man oh man, I guess I really am."

"You're just trying to put one over."

"I wish I were."

"Yahoo!" Sam yelled as he gave the motor a kick start and then some gas.

———

He had many, many conversations with Krista, but they were all in his head. He thought he saw her everywhere but it was never her, it was always another girl with short brown hair.

"Loon! How's it going?"

He turned, stopped fiddling with the combination lock on his locker, and began to tremble inside. It *was* her. "How's it going?" he said.

"That's just what I asked you." She smiled, eye level. They were the same height. Maybe she had on heels. No, they wore the same running shoes.

He began to grope for words. "Uh . . . uh . . ."

"Are you practicing a lot?"

"Sort of. I wish it was over. *Were* over."

"Oh, don't worry. You'll do fine."

"Mmm."

"See ya." She gave his arm a little squeeze and disappeared into the crowd. A hot spot remained where her hand had been.

"Gee," said Sam. "She's a junior and I think she likes you. How come you didn't say anything."

He'd forgotten Sam was standing beside him. "I did."

"Well, I hope you do better than that in the contest."

"Thanks."

All through geometry he thought how he could've done better. When she said "you practicing a lot?" he should've said "you mean baseball?" Opportunity knocked and he hadn't answered.

Yes, he was practicing a lot. He could've told her the

truth, how he once picked up the phone and said "kak" instead of "hello." After all, it probably didn't matter. To her he was Loon. How much worse could it get?

"Give me a few on the ground." Eric punched his glove and bent forward with his hands on his knees.

He and Sam were tossing the ball back and forth along the third base line, warming up before their game against the Wildcats. He was psyched up for this game. He was ready to beat the pants off the Wildcats.

"Hey!" Eric shouted. "I said on the ground!" He leaped for the ball, which was about to sail over his head. Pop. Right into the webbing. He dug the ball from his glove and coiled his arm back to toss a fly ball. But right in the middle of his throw he turned his head toward a grove of trees set back from the field. Slowly he brought his arm down and stood motionless. He was listening, waiting to hear it again.

"Weesee weesee weesee weesee weesee . . . tchack tchack tchack . . . whit-wheet! . . . whit-wheet! . . . weesee weesee weesee . . . swee swee . . . swee swee. . . ."

"What're you doing? Throw me the ball!" Sam kicked at the ground with his spike.

"Waitasecond, hush." Eric lowered his head and closed his eyes, straining to hear.

"Seet seet seet . . . trrrr . . . swee swee. . . ."

No kidding, that was a nice sound. "It's some sort of mockingbird," he said mostly to himself. "I never heard one before. Man oh man. Listen!"

"Hey, *throw* the ball *back*."

"All right, all right." Eric gripped the ball with two fingers and lobbed it back to Sam. It dropped a few feet in front of him on the ground.

"Nice throw. Are you ready or what?" Sam picked up the ball and tossed it up into the air above his head, catching it himself. Twice, three times. "Hey, you in birdland! *Catch!*" He hurled it at Eric. *"Eric!"*

But it was too late. Eric's head was turned toward the grove of trees. He never saw the ball. It struck him just under the left eyebrow, also catching his upper cheekbone and the left side of his nose. He staggered a few feet backward, tore his glove off and dropped to the ground.

"I'm sorry, I'm sorry!" Sam ran to him, kneeled, and tilted his head back. "Gosh, I'm sorry, Eric, I thought you'd catch it. Let's see . . . oh *man*."

"Ohhh," said Eric, "ahhhhh. . . ."

"You're not bleeding. Not much. It's mostly just red and, well, swelling a bit. But where'd your eye go? Hey, just kidding. We'll put some ice on it. You'll be all right."

"See see . . ." said Eric.

"What?"

"See see . . ."

"See what, man?" Sam waved his hand back and forth in front of Eric's eyes. "You can see me, can't you, buddy?"

"See see see see see Miss Beech'er."

"Oh my God. . . ."

"See see see see see Miss Beech'er."

"It's not Miss Beech'er, Eric. It's me."

". . . see Miss Beech'er . . ."

"It's me, Sam. Is that her last name, Eric? Beecher? Don't call her 'Miss,' it's old-fashioned. I bet she's gone home, so you can't see her anyway. I'm sorry, and stop whistling. It's not the seventeenth of March. You should stop eating that birdseed. *Hey! Somebody get us some ice!*"

Eric stood at the foot of his bed, gazing absently at the yellow sweats spread across it. He was going to wear them in the contest, along with black greasepaint on his face and a gray rinse in his hair.

He gingerly put a finger to his left eye, which was swollen half shut. Around it his face was a swirl of color. Opportunity had knocked him on the head instead of on the mouth, where it would have counted. This morning the members of his family came pecking at his bedroom door one by one. First his mom. Did he want breakfast in bed? Was he going to school? Then his dad. Could he get him some aspirin, more ice? Finally, his sister came towing Tu by the hand. "Monster face," said Tu. He'd only gotten more attention when he'd broken his wrist in a skateboarding mishap.

He began to pace the length of his room. He looked at his watch. It was 7:17 P.M. In less than twenty hours the Seventeenth of March Annual Birdcalling Contest and Brouhaha would be underway. The brouhaha was a party and dance following the contest, with a live band outside behind the school. Actually, he thought, *brouhaha* sounded more like the name of a rare South American bird.

He looked at his watch. It was 7:22 P.M. His stomach began to flutter. He got down on the floor and began to do sit-ups. One, two, three, four. . . . He did fifty and looked at his watch: 7:28 P.M. He got up, unzipped his backpack, and carried his U.S. History II book to his bed. The fluttering in his stomach continued. It felt like a little bird. He should not have eaten so many seeds and raisins.

Maybe it was a bird. Maybe the egg he'd had for breakfast had hatched, come home to roost. He had the sudden and strange sensation that all he would have to do tomorrow afternoon was open his mouth, and it would sing.

One by one the participants' names were called and the cluster of kids backstage grew smaller and smaller. The audience went wild for the Siberian red-tailed shrike and the veery, because of its loud staccato "teacher teacher teacher." He saw some clever costumes and heard several exceptional singers.

He stood backstage on feet like blocks of ice. He did not have to worry about mucus. His mouth was so dry his tongue had fused to the top of his mouth. He sipped from a bottle of mineral water and tried to continue breathing.

Finally, his name was called and he strode out to center stage on his clumps of ice. Out past the white glaring lights was a sea of faces, among them his family, friends, Jordan and Lawrence, and Krista. He took a deep breath, trying to remember everything Anthony had taught him. Then he placed himself behind the podium with his feet spread slightly apart and his hands clenched behind his back. It was not unlike stepping into the batter's box with the bases loaded and two outs in the bottom of the ninth.

He shut his eyes and forgot about all the people waiting to hear him. He forgot about the bet with Lawrence and the TV cameras and reporters and everything else. He let all the air escape from his lungs and inhaled as deeply as he could. Then, for about sixty seconds, he became his main bird, Lawrence's goldfinch.

"You see, when you figure out who you really are, when you're able to be yourself, things fall into place." He'd just finished telling Jordan the story of the finches and jays. Now he dug a tissue from his back pocket and blew his nose. He was back to eating mucus-producing foods, although he'd acquired a taste for raisins and seeds. "I was always wanting to be kind of a tough guy, but it wasn't really me."

"If I figure out who I am, will I be able to go on the David Letterman show like you?" asked Jordan. He and Eric were sitting on Eric's front porch. It was the twenty-ninth of March.

"Well, I guess that depends on who you *are*. I was just lucky. Hammer is really a nice guy, by the way. Very down-to-earth. I felt pretty silly doing the bird songs in front of him, but he said if he ever needed bird songs in a recording he'd give me a call."

"We taped it on our VCR," said Jordan. "Dad keeps watching it over and over. He still has that newspaper article on his desk too."

Eric knew the article from the *Chronicle* word for word. It said:

> Looking like nobody's "tweetie pie" because of an apparent missed fastball to his face, Eric Randall-Pena "tink-oo'ed" and "ti-dee-di-di-ed" his way to at least local fame and a modest $150 fortune in Friday's Seventeenth of March Annual Birdcalling Contest and Brouhaha. Held at Oakland's Eastmont High School before its annual spring Brouhaha, the contest featured the best in local chirpers. Mr. Randall-Pena, alias Lawrence's goldfinch . . .

"I couldn't believe I was there either. Get that gicky stuff off your face, Jordan. What is it this time, Three Musketeers?"

"It's . . . bet you a dollar . . . oh, forget it. I don't have a dollar."

"Neither do I. Nobody's paid me yet."

"Not even my dad?"

"No. I *could* let him off the hook, since I've been offered that $8,500 advertising job with the Sure Sing Bird Supply Company. But I don't think I will. I believe it's the last bet he'll ever make with me."

"Were you scared?"

"Naaa . . ." Eric cracked a knuckle and smiled. "Yeah. More than ever in my life. I'm glad it's over."

"What are you going to do with the money?"

"Buy a pair of good binoculars. Save the rest for college."

"Eric, what kind of a bird do you think I am?" Jordan pulled another Mallo Cup from his shirt pocket and began to rip off the paper. "Want some?"

"Uh huh. Hmmm, let's see. I'd say a white-rumped sandpiper."

"*Eeeeeeeee!*" Jordan screeched. "No, really!"

Eric laughed. "Okay, for sure you're a bobwhite. It's like a little chicken, just like you, Jordan."

"Oh," Jordan said flatly. "Well, I ain't white, Eric."

"So? I ain't gold, am I? We're talking personality, not color."

"Do you suppose you could teach me, you know. . . ."

"Yeah, if we don't tell your dad."

"Look who's coming. You've got all the luck."

Eric swallowed. He still swallowed every time he saw her. "It's not luck, I'm telling you. Be yourself."

"A bobwhite. I'm not telling my dad."

"Hi." Eric smiled as Krista turned and headed up his sidewalk. *His* sidewalk. He dug into his back pocket for an article he'd clipped from the *Chronicle* and wanted to show her. It was a true story about a young woman, Gwendolyn Grater, who married a ferruginous hawk up in Yreka in 1917. Her parents had it immediately annulled by a Judge Boise Threepenny. Eric thought it was hilarious.

"Hi, Eric." She smiled back, coming to stand right

beside him. The little flecks of brown and gold and gray in her eyes flickered and danced in the sun. As she laid a hand on his shoulder and smiled, he wondered how her parents felt about finches.

"How's my sweet bird of youth?" she asked.

His heart swelled like a giant balloon in his chest, until it seemed to carry him up, up somewhere high above the steps. He, Lawrence's goldfinch, was soaring, lighter than air, looking down on his life with a big smile, "Ti-dee-di-di . . . ti-dee-di-di . . . ti-dee-di-di. . . ."

Tu
Eyes

*T*u sat on a small stool near the opening to the big tent. He slept in the big tent with the mom and dad. The brother, Eric, and the sister, Lindsey, slept in the small tent. Small tent, big tent. Big tent, small tent. He was learning new words.

He looked down at his feet. His shoelace was untied. The flap hung open like a big red tongue. He stuck out his own tongue to see how far it would go. He could see it if he looked straight down. It was pink, not red. There was that shoelace again, still untied. Someone ought to tie it. He would ask the mom when she finished changing clothes in the big green tent.

Trin from the school did not tell him that the new mother and father would be tall as trees. He had seen pictures when he was still with his uncle Lo. He knew that their eyes would be round as seashells and their hair the color of tea. But some things you cannot know from a picture.

The mother came out of the big tent. He stuck out his red shoe and said, "Please."

"Someday you will do this yourself, Tu." She knelt, looked up at him and smiled.

"I carry water myself," said Tu.

"That's right," she answered. "You're a good helper. Would you like to get some now, so we have water to put out the campfire?"

He nodded. Then he picked up the plastic water jug and started up the path.

In these woods the trunks of the trees were red. He stopped and turned his face up to the sky, where the treetops crowded together. When he got to be bigger he would climb a red tree to see the sky up close.

He passed the funny little building called an outhouse on the way to the pump. You could be outside a house. You could be inside a house. How could you be *inside* an outhouse? Ever since Eric made him watch a movie called *The Fly*, he did not like using the outhouse.

As he filled the jug with water he hummed a song to himself, "Hmmm mmmm mm mm mm mm." It was a song his uncle Lo used to sing, but he could not remember the words. Sometimes he even forgot what his uncle looked like. He shut his eyes and tried to see him now.

"Tu! The water's running over!"

It was not his uncle's face but sister Lindsey's. He quickly twisted the knob of the faucet. He picked up the container of water, but it was now very heavy.

"Here, I'll help you," said Lindsey.

Tu said no. He had told Mother he would carry the water. He would carry the water.

"It's really heavy," said Lindsey.

Tu began to drag the water jug away from the pump.

"You're Tu Stubborn," said Lindsey. "You should let me help you." She shook her head and looked at him as though she were puzzled.

Back in his old home he only had one name. Tu Ng. It was short. It was easy. Here he had many. Tu Stubborn. Tu Dirty. Tu Grumpy. Earlier today Father had looked at him in a swimming suit and said he was Tu Skinny. He didn't like his American names. Someday I will go back across the ocean and just be Tu again, he promised himself. He, Tu Stubborn, would carry his own suitcase.

As he dragged the water down the path Lindsey trailed behind like the scruffy old dog he used to love back home.

"You should let me help you," she said again and again. He stopped to wipe the dust from his eyes and nose, and to secretly rest his sore shoulders and arms. But he wouldn't let her help.

When they returned to their campsite the mother was lighting the campfire. Soon the flames were leaping up toward the darkening sky. Eric and Lindsey shoved sharp sticks through marshmallows and stuck them into the fire. Eric let Tu hold a stick until the marshmallow burst into flames.

"Can we have some chocolate too?" asked Lindsey.

"How should I know?" said Tu. Questions, questions. He heard his name all day long. "Should we bring the bats too?" "Should we try to hike tomorrow too?" Did they think he had all the answers? He was only four after all.

He pulled a string of marshmallow hanging from his chin and pushed it into his mouth. The fire gave this family strange funny faces. The father looked like a cat. The mother looked like an owl. The brother and sister were monsters. For a long time he hadn't liked to look at their faces. Now he could look, but he wasn't always sure he knew the people inside the faces.

Now which one was that? Two marshmallow eyes behind the owl and the cat. He counted. The owl, the cat, two monsters, and . . . "One, two, three, four, five," he said out loud.

"That's good, Tu," said Lindsey. "Try to count to ten."

"One, two, three, four, five," he said, going around the circle again.

"Practice makes perfect," said Eric.

"One, two," said Tu. "Tu eyes behind you."

The owl, the cat, and the monsters laughed.

"Tu eyes behind you," he repeated. This time he pointed to the pair of white eyes gleaming in the darkness.

The mother turned, saw two eyes over her shoulder, and screamed. She threw up her hands and fell off the tree stump. The father turned, saw two eyes, and yelled, "AAAAAAAAH!" He fell off the tree stump.

Tu began to cry. Tu Eyes had got them. They were dead. He began to cry harder. *"Eo-meo-ni, a-beo-ji,"* he cried. They were the olds words for mother and father. He had almost forgotten.

But then his parents got up. They brushed the dirt from their hands and legs, laughing about the big raccoon, which had now disappeared. Then Tu's father lifted him up and squeezed him very tightly. He felt lost and little in his father's arms but he didn't care, because Tu Eyes had not got him. Tu Eyes had not got his mother either. It was funny. First he was crying, now he was laughing. First his *eo-meo-ni* and *a-beo-ji* were laughing, now they were crying.

"You are Tu Wonderful," cried his mother. She pressed her cheek to his forehead.

Maybe. But that wasn't what they called him. From then on he was Tu Eyes.

Birds of a Feather

*J*ordan stood on the ledge of the bathtub pointing an imaginary .22 caliber rifle into the mirror above the sink. He took aim, squeezing his left eye shut. "You're one dead quail!" he said, and then pulled the trigger. "Bam! Gotcha!"

He removed the butt of the imaginary rifle from his shoulder and was about to reload for another imaginary round when his father, Lawrence, rapped on the bathroom door.

"Get a move on," he called. "If I can't get you up in the morning I'll have to leave you behind."

Jordan's father was taking him hunting for the first time in his life. Jordan was thrilled. He could hardly wait. Hopping off the ledge of the bathtub, he yanked open the door and marched down the hall with the imaginary rifle slung over his real shoulder.

He wasn't so excited when his dad shook him awake at 5:30 the next morning. He shivered as he removed his pajamas and fumbled his way into jeans and a sweater. He staggered sleepily to the car in the driveway and crawled into the front seat. Lawrence slammed the trunk shut and heaved himself into the seat beside Jordan.

"I hope this fog clears," said Lawrence. That was the only thing he said for fifteen minutes, until they turned off Highway 680 and swung east out toward the foothills. Then they ate crunchy blueberry granola from a paper bag. Lawrence sipped coffee from a thermos. Every so often Jordan would raise his imaginary gun and take aim at something along the roadside. "Ping. Zap. Gotcha."

Sunlight filtered through the fog as Jordan's father parked the car where the road dead-ended at a clump of blue oak trees. The fog also was lifting in Jordan's head. He hopped out of the car and leaped for a low-hanging tree branch, swinging back and forth as he hung by his hands.

He watched his father stuff some cartridges into the

pockets of his hunting jacket, then sling the gun strap across his shoulder. He also slipped a pair of binoculars around his neck. "Jordan," he called.

Jordan dropped from the tree and came running. He took the backpack from his dad and slid it onto his back. When he was older he'd carry a gun like his dad.

They started off, with Jordan following his father along the narrow dirt path that cut through the scrub oak, blue oak, manzanita, and eucalyptus trees. "Hep, hep, hep two three four . . . hep, hep . . ."

"Jordan," said Lawrence. "Don't scare off the game."

"Oh, yeah," said Jordan. "Right." Falling into step with his dad he began to sing to himself. Hep, hep, hep two three four . . . He squinted against the reflection of sunlight off the barrel of the gun slung across his father's back. He wondered how far they would have to walk before they got to use it.

. . . Hep, hep two three . . . They could be soldiers going off to battle, he and his dad . . . four, hep, hep . . .

"Quail flush at about fifty yards," said Lawrence, half turning to whisper to Jordan.

Jordan nodded but he didn't know what that meant. In his mind he saw a big bird squawking and flailing about as it swirled around the bottom of a toilet bowl. But that wasn't right. "How many do you think we'll get?" he whispered back.

Lawrence shrugged and, turning again, put his finger to his lips. That meant no more talking.

Jordan had a lot of questions but they would have to

wait. Later he'd ask his dad if he was a good shot. How old was he when he killed his first bird? What did you do with it after you shot it? What happened when you . . . *"Yeow!"* He yelled, his head snapping up toward a sound that was like an explosion.

The tree ahead of them had burst apart! The sky above it was a flurry of wings!

Lawrence grabbed his binoculars. "Wow!" he said. "That's a covey of quail. Now you've seen one."

In a second the quail had all flown away and it was dead silent. As he again fell into step behind his dad, Jordan wondered how they were going to shoot something that moved so fast. Underneath his boots the flattened, sun-yellowed grass snapped and crunched. He lifted his right boot to kick a stone and changed his mind. Good thing. He might have scared off the game. Who knew what was in the bushes and trees just up ahead.

His father suddenly stopped, raising the binoculars to gaze across the field. "Junco," he whispered. "I dunno. Maybe not." Then he lowered the binoculars and started moving again.

"We're closing in on the creek bed," he said a short time later, shading his eyes against the sun. "Quail really like creek beds because they've got water and underbrush and stuff to hide in."

"How do they know they'll be hunted?"

"It's instinct. They're born knowing. So even baby quail know to hide out in bushes. Some stuff they learn from other birds. Shssh." Lawrence put a finger to his lips and pointed. A bush ahead was stirring even though no wind was blowing. "Quail," he silently mouthed. Very slowly he raised the binoculars and peered through them. Then he removed a few shells from his pocket and loaded the chamber. He motioned for Jordan to follow.

Jordan tried to swallow but he had a lump in his throat that wouldn't go down. As they crept along the path, he began to get the jitters. He wasn't sure why. Maybe it was waiting for that bush to explode again and you didn't know when it would . . . maybe it was wondering what a dead . . . *bam!*

"*Ahhhh!*" he yelped, covering his ears. This explosion was right in his ear. The empty shell dropped from his father's gun to the ground. Startled birds plunged from tree to tree shrieking.

"I think I missed," said Lawrence, "Oh, well. See how fast they are and how they flock together. See, see?"

Jordan was glad his father was not upset about missing his shot. Maybe he wouldn't be mad at him if he missed too. "When can I try?" he asked bravely, no longer sure he wanted to.

"We'll see," replied Lawrence. He was focusing the binoculars again, studying the birds still crisscrossing the sky.

"These aren't quail?" asked Jordan, looking upward.

"No. You'll get to know the difference. Hmm. I see another junco. Two juncos and a finch of some sort. Finches, ha!"

Since these weren't quail Jordan took a good swipe at

a stone with his foot. The sun was on its way up the sky now and he was thirsty. He could hear and feel the juice sloshing around the inside of a thermos on his back.

"Well, let's keep moving," said Lawrence. He slung the gun back over his shoulder and headed down the slope of the hill.

Jordan now noticed that he was not much taller than the gun on his father's shoulder. He'd never picked it up but he supposed it was heavy. Shooting didn't look hard but maybe it was. It wasn't like basketball. You couldn't just practice your shots in the driveway. He remembered a shooting gallery at a carnival in his school yard. You hit the ducks with a BB and down they went. It was fun.

He should've thought of this before but now he tried to remember what people looked like shooting guns on television. He knew his father would teach him how to do it but he didn't want to look like a total jerk.

"Here we are."

Jordan stood next to his father, looking down the creek bank at a stream swirling and gurgling around some rocks.

"If we hang around here, the quail will come to us," said Lawrence. He leaned the gun against a tree and eased himself to the ground. Then he raised the binoculars and scanned the bushes and trees lining the other side of the creek bed.

Jordan bent to pick up a roundish brown thing that looked like a big acorn off the ground. "What is it?" he asked, rolling it around in his hand.

"Buckeye. We're sitting under a buckeye tree."

"I thought buckeye was ammunition, something you shot deer with." He looked up at the tree towering above them, its branches stretching up and away like someone's long arms.

"That's buck*shot*," said Lawrence. "Take the pack off. Let's eat something. If you look closely at the buckeye, you'll see why it's called that."

Jordan sat down, wiggling free of the pack. He examined the buckeye again, it's "eye" staring up at him from the palm of his hand.

"A buck's a male deer. That's why buckshot is called buckshot. It's really lead."

"Are there deer out here?"

"Sure. We might see some droppings, look like little pebbles."

"You ever shot one?"

"Nope. Don't like venison."

"What's venison?"

"Deer meat. Want half a sandwich?"

"Yeah. Why don't they call it 'deer' then, like chicken or rabbit?"

"Things aren't always called what they are. Would you like bacon, ham, or pig for breakfast? See what I mean?"

"Pig and eggs," said Jordan, laughing. He slipped the buckeye into his left jacket pocket and began to unwrap his sandwich.

"Some people get so excited the first time they go hunting and see game, they get buck fever." Lawrence balanced his sandwich on his knee, still peering through the binoculars. "They can't do anything right. They're beside themselves with excitement. They're wild. They miss every shot."

"You ever had buck fever?"

"Nope."

Jordan peered under the top slice of bread. "Pig sandwich," he said, sinking his teeth into it.

Lawrence smiled.

Jordan had barely begun to chew when the underbrush down the creek began to rustle and stir. Lawrence cocked his head toward the sound. Very slowly he raised the binoculars and adjusted the lens with two fingers. Without a sound he slipped them off his neck and handed them over to Jordan.

Jordan could see a spotty gray bird with a little round head, which it was scratching with a spindly leg, like a cat or dog would. It opened and closed its beak in song, "Chica'-go, Chi-ca'-go, Chi-ca'-go."

Lawrence swung the gun around in front of him, pointed, and fired. Jordan refused to cover his ears this time, even waited for his dad to take another shot, but he didn't. He leaned the gun against the tree and raised the binoculars instead. The covey was long gone anyway.

"Oh, well," he said. "I still don't think I hit anything."

How could he, thought Jordan, aiming way over their heads like that. He didn't think it was buck fever either, because his dad went hunting all the time. But he jumped up onto his feet anyway, offering to go see if there was a bird down just in case. He hopped across the shallow creek on some of the flatter rocks and scuffed around in the dirt a bit. Secretly relieved that he did not have to pick up a dead quail, he spun around and hopped across the rocks again.

Scrambling up the steep creek side he wondered what his dad did with all the quail he shot. And pheasant and duck. How come he never brought them home for dinner?

His father was sipping coffee from his thermos, nibbling on a Hostess cupcake. "Did we get one?" he absently asked.

"Nope." Surely his dad could see that. Where would he be hiding a dead quail? In his underpants?

Then his father licked his fingers one by one and lay back onto the yellowed grass with his hand underneath his head and his feet crossed. "You know what?" he said.

"What?" Jordan sat down beside him cross-legged on the hard dry ground.

"Some scientists think that birds can hear the sound of waves crashing on a shore thousands of miles away."

"No," Jordan replied. "That's impossible."

"Kid you not. I read it. That kind of hearing helps them migrate. That's nature for you. Yo, thrush," he called softly, gazing up at the buckeye tree. "Yo, thrush."

"You got some cupcake on your lip, Dad," said Jordan.

Lawrence wiped a crumpled napkin across his mouth. "My ma had a bird feeder in the backyard. She used to sit at the window, which was just about the length of a broom handle from the ground, and shoo the neighborhood cats—and once my friend Daryl who got a Daisy air rifle for his birthday. She'd sit and sit and sit watching the birds come and go. Say, you know who's got the biggest bird feeder in the city? Bet you five bucks you can't guess it."

Jordan twisted a long yellow weed around his left thumb, thinking, then around his right thumb, thinking. Bird feeder, bird feeder, bird feeder. "The zoo?" he tried hopefully. He started in on the rest of his sandwich, stuffing the little plastic baggie into the pack.

"Nope. Guess again?"

"Have I seen it?"

"Many, many times. I'll tell you." He raised his head and grinned. "It's McDonald's."

"What?"

"That's right. Burger King too. They wait for the crumbs—you never saw so many birds. Watch when we go again. All the little sparrows."

His dad let his head fall back again, smiling. He never looked like this at home, thought Jordan, like his face was putty, could melt right into the grass underneath his head.

"Hey, look," said Lawrence. He pointed up at the sky.

A trio of red-tailed hawks glided and swooped in circles high above them. Jordan watched the hawks with his dad for a while, until they were smudges in the distant sky. Then he said, "Dad, how come we never eat quail?"

"Well," said his father, sighing. "It's because I never

shot a thing. That's the truth. Never shot a bird in my life, probably never will."

"That's what I thought," said Jordan. He got up and ran across the meadow to the top of a little hill. For a moment he just stood there, feeling a little disappointed about not taking a shot. Maybe he'd still get a chance and he'd aim high like his dad. Blame it on "buck fever." His dad wouldn't care if he ever hit a thing. That made him suddenly happy and relieved. He felt so light inside. He took off running. He was a hawk and the meadow beneath him the sky. He ran and ran, lifting his arms and flapping them gently like imaginary wings.

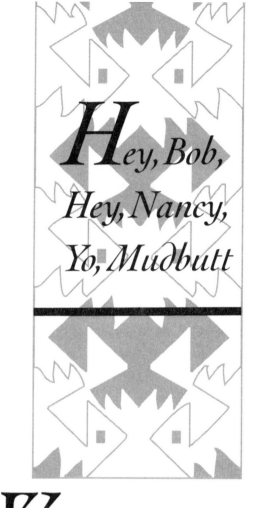

*H*ey, Bob, Hey, Nancy, Yo, Mudbutt

*W*ho was Ms. Azumba kidding? How could you start writing and not know what you were going to say? Lindsey stared at the piece of white lined paper on her desk. If she looked at it hard enough and long enough it began to look like a window. But a window to what, or to where?

She slid her right foot out of its loafer and bent to scratch an itch on her arch. Ms. Azumba said writing was like cooking. She said that thoughts were like separate ingredients in a recipe — they wouldn't mean much until you began to stir them together. One thought led to another and another and pretty soon you'd really be "cooking." If that were true, her mind was an empty oven.

Just start with any old thing, she told herself, but she couldn't. Not really. She couldn't just write "the" and "this" and "me" and "desk" and "shoes" and "brown" and "potato." Potato? Now where did *that* word come from? "Me and this desk and the brown potato." It wasn't even a complete sentence. I just don't have anything to say, she thought sadly, putting her pen down.

Lindsey rubbed her nose, pulled on her earlobe, and wiped the back of her hand across her forehead as she tried to turn the heat up in her mind. She was a good writer and she knew it. Thus, she had a hard time understanding her difficulty with the assignment. Usually she chose a topic, made an outline, wrote the essay. That wasn't working.

Once again she glanced up at the chalkboard, on which the word "essay" was printed in large yellow letters. Except that Ms. Azumba had written "es-SAY," because, she said, "when you write an essay, you *say* something. "Es-SAY." Learn to *say* what you think and feel and see. Learn to *commun*-icate. *Commune*, it means together. Remember that you are saying something to each one of us." She'd waved her arms as though the class were a choir, ready to burst into song.

Lindsey fingered the curled corner of her blank sheet

of paper. Brown potato, she said to them all. Brown potato in my shoe.

Under the word "es-SAY" on the blackboard were three choices:

> If I were . . .
> I wish I . . .
> I'm glad I'm not . . .

Lindsey reread the choices again and again. Many ideas passed through her mind. *If I were on a sinking ship, how would I spend my last hour? I wish I had lived in the 1960s because . . . I wish I could live for a year in Venice, Italy . . . I'm glad I'm not Amish because . . .* These and other ideas passed through her mind and then out again. The pot was still empty.

She wiped her sweaty writing hand on her knee. This cooking stuff was hard. She usually wrote a paragraph for every major heading in her outline. That way you knew where you were going, like following a recipe line by line. This way you could end up anywhere. It was too risky. She wanted an *A*.

Potato.

It was like a little gnat buzzing in her mind, and she said, No, go away, that's goofy. Just because writing is like cooking doesn't mean you have to write about food. She squirmed in her chair, a small panic rising with the clicking of the clock. She looked around the walls of the room for help. There on the wall, a calendar for May, a photo of undersea life. If I were a seahorse . . . , she tried. If I were a seahorse . . .

Removing the chewed-up end of the pencil from her mouth, she wrote the word *seahorse* over and over. When you did this the thoughts were supposed to start bubbling up to the surface of your mind. Seahorse seahorse seahorse. Perhaps hers were trapped beneath an air pocket because she had nothing to say. She could say something about her desk though. One leg was shorter than the others and it wobbled and rocked when she squirmed. It was rocking now, *clack clack clack* against the floor. Several kids turned and frowned to let her know.

"Tick . . . tick . . . tick . . . tick . . ."

She put her pencil to paper, feeling desperate. Just write anything, anything, *anything. If I were an Amish seahorse on a ship sinking in Venice . . .*

Her ship was sinking all right. She swiveled toward the back of the room to see her friends Tosh and Lorry writing furiously on pages that appeared nearly full. Well great. Everyone had something to say but her. If her paper was a window, she wanted to crawl through it.

Time to get down to business. "I'm glad I'm not a brown potato," she wrote. "If I were a brown potato I'd be headed for trouble. . . ." Trouble is . . . she sighed as she put down her pencil and wiped her hand on her pants. I *am* headed for trouble.

One more time. She picked up her pencil, hunched over her paper, and waited. Maybe with her head down a thought dislodged in the back would roll forward, and then another and another, like in dominoes. She readied her pencil in her hand and waited. Finally her hand moved. "Potato," it wrote. She sighed, biting her lower lip. That's it? she said to herself.

She kept her head down but raised her eyes, only to meet the inquiring gaze of Ms. Azumba, who was seated behind her desk. Lindsey pressed her lips together and began to write furiously. "Potato potato potato," she wrote. "Brown brown brown brown brown shoe shoe desk desk this is a mess." Well, it didn't say anything, but it had rhythm. Her father, a journalist with the *Oakland Tribune*, went for long walks to get over his writer's blocks. She wondered if Ms. Azumba would grant her permission to take one. Ha-ha. This wasn't funny. She really was sweating and her heart was pounding hard. Thumpa thumpa thumpa.

"Brrrrrrnnnnnngggggg!" She flew three inches up off her chair as the buzzer jolted the classroom into a commotion.

Ms. Azumba rose to her feet, removing her black-rimmed glasses. "Please put your essays on my desk as you line up. I'll look them over and you can finish them on Monday. Quickly! Quickly! Move in an orderly fashion!"

Oh, no, thought Lindsey. She peeled the single damp sheet of paper from the surface of her desk. Ms. Azumba was going to "look them over" before Monday. Who was she kidding? She would *read* every single one of them.

It seemed cold for May. With her friends Lorry and Tosh, Lindsey huddled in an alcove between two wings of the old stucco school building. The wind had dried the perspiration on her back. She reached underneath her jacket to pull her shirt away from her clammy skin, just as she had peeled the damp sheet of paper off of her desk. "How are you guys doing?" she asked.

"All right." Lorry shivered, leaning against a letter *L* scrawled in red across the faded yellow stucco, her hands deep in the pockets of her jeans. "How're you doing?"

"I mean on the essay."

"Oh, it's sort of fun, isn't it? I'm doing 'I wish I were a talk show host.' Not like Johnny Carson, you know. More sophisticated than that. I think I'd be good at drawing people out, asking the right questions, you know?"

"Yeah, you would." Lindsey watched in curious amazement as Tosh, one knee on the pavement, fumbled around the inside of her backpack, which bulged and strained at its seams.

"I listed some of the people I'd interview."

"You'd finally get paid money for talking, instead of just little checkmarks on your report card," said Tosh. She opened a small paperback dictionary—"Mmm, got it right"—and tossed it back into her pack. "I'm doing a story about trekking through the Himalayas. I read an article about it once. The Sherpa guides carry your packs. Or is it donkeys?"

"The Sherpas carry donkeys?" said Lindsey. "Wow." She smiled at Lorry.

"Silly!" Tosh cried.

"You'd need a Sherpa and a donkey," said Lorry.

"Snots!" Tosh pulled a beaded bracelet from her pack and eased it onto her dark slender wrist.

They used snot as a term of endearment, referring to themselves as the Snot Sisters since the fourth grade, when Patty Jablonski called them a bunch of snots for hiding her naked Barbie doll in Keith Corona's day pack. Last year they had T-shirts made with SNOT SISTERS on the front and a personalized EARTHA, BERTHA, or MERTHA on the back. Lindsey was Bertha Snot and her parents didn't much care for the name or the shirt.

"What are you writing about, Lindsey?" Tosh asked absently.

"Well . . . it's . . . I'm . . . 'I'm glad I'm not . . .' " She stuffed her hands into her jacket pockets, pulled a chocolate kiss from her right-hand pocket, and unwrapped it. The silvery paper reminded her of tinsel, wrapping foil, holidays. She wished today had been one.

Stuff from Tosh's bag spilled onto the pavement. A barrette. Gum. Change purse. Rubber bands. A quarter rolled in circles, around and around.

"Glad you're not what?" Lorry slid her back down the wall to sit cross-legged on the pavement.

Lindsey popped the kiss into her mouth. She liked to eat sugar when she was worried. "A potato," she mumbled.

"Yeah?" Now Tosh was down on both knees, picking up more things that had fallen. A brown banana. Sunglasses. Paperback novel. Super Glue. Walkman.

They hadn't really heard her. That was good. She didn't feel like explaining how the word *potato* had popped into her head, and couldn't explain it anyway.

"You're like a bag lady," she said to Tosh.

"No, I'm not. A bag lady would've eaten the banana."

"Yeah. That's right." She shivered as the first gray curl of fog passed high overhead, her arms wrapped around her chest and the chocolate kiss flat on her tongue. "She probably wouldn't have a Walkman either," she noted, remembering the woman in rags by the Avenue Eatery.

"What're you doing tomorrow?" asked Tosh. "Want to go to a movie, go shopping?"

"Sure," replied Lindsey and Lorry, as the bell rang, ending recess. Lindsey reached for her day pack.

"*Potatoes!*" Tosh suddenly repeated, grunting as she hurled her bag onto her shoulder. She turned to shake her head at Lindsey. "You're such a *goon*!"

She usually enjoyed Friday afternoons because she loved both art period and the free library hour. But on this particular day she sensed a dark foreboding cloud drifting toward her in the shape of a large brown potato.

Lindsey examined the baked potato on her dinner plate. It was smothered in margarine with a dab of sour cream on each half. Normally she loved baked potatoes. This one gave her the creeps.

She was only half tuned in to the conversation between her parents because she was still worried about her "es-SAY," now in the hands of Ms. Azumba. She *liked* Ms.

Azumba, who was from Kenya, Africa. She was perhaps the best teacher she'd ever had. Mrs. Marks in the fifth grade had been among the worst. She sometimes fell asleep during oral book reports, and the legs of her panty hose were twisted and bumpy like two relief maps of California. Mr. Mendelsohn, seventh grade, was not bad, but he became preoccupied with paper origami as the year went on and finally had a nervous breakdown in March, which parents referred to as an "adult stress reaction."

On one or two occasions Ms. Azumba had complimented Lindsey on her writing. She did not want to disappoint Ms. Azumba. By Monday she would come up with a great idea. "I wish I were . . ." "I'm glad I'm not . . ." She turned the phrases over in her mind as she poked a slice of tomato with her fork.

"So I'm trying to wrap up my project"—her mother, Anne, reached across the table to slice her brother Tu's red snapper—"and this guy Howard in the next office keeps coming back to me asking for this and that and you name it."

"He's not your supervisor or anything, right?" asked Lindsey's father.

"No, he's not anything. I mean, nobody knows *what* he does. He's sort of a jerk. And I *told* him I had a deadline."

"Next time tell him to get lost. That's what I'd do." Her father winked at Lindsey and handed her the basket of bread.

"Yeah, maybe I will. He just thinks he's, you know, a real hot potato or something."

Lindsey threw a suspicious glance toward her mother.

"Tell him," her father suggested, "that if he doesn't quit bugging you, you'll *mash* his potatoes." He and Lindsey's mother laughed. Lindsey harpooned a tiny piece of garlic and squirmed in her chair.

"He's only half baked anyway," said Anne. They were very entertained by their own little jokes, chuckling in between bites of food.

Lindsey slid forward to the edge of her chair and sunk her fork into the mound of sour cream. Steam rose from beneath it. Then she saw a vision. It was a little face in the baked potato. No, it could not be a face. Yes, it was. Whose face? Hers. No, not *her* face. Yes, no mistaking it, that was her nose, her eyes, her mouth.

"Lindsey, you're not laughing. Gee, you're not eating either. Is anything wrong?"

Lindsey could see the sheet of white paper on her desk. She could see the word she had written, "potato."

"I won't do it," she cried.

Her mom tilted her head in a worrisome way. Her father pursed his lips.

"That's all right," said Anne, laying her hand on Lindsey's shoulder. "Is the potato hard in the center? I could toss it in the microwave."

Lindsey shook her head. How could she explain this? And what was going on here anyway, some sort of junior high stress reaction?

"I hate how everyone says teenagers hang out in malls," said Lorry. She sat in the backseat next to Lindsey. It was Saturday afternoon. They were on their way to see a matinee at the Hilltop Shopping Center, and they were wearing their SNOT SISTERS T-shirts.

"We don't hang out in malls," Lorry continued. "We just go once in a while. But every time we go I feel guilty, like Barbara Walters or Mike Wallace will be there with their camera crews. If I were a talk show host it's not a story I'd bother with."

"I once heard age thirteen called the tweenage," said Lindsey. She lifted herself an inch off the seat and pulled down on the legs of her jeans. They were too tight because she'd eaten too many corn chips with her tuna sandwich.

"Tweenagers. Tween what?" said Tosh, turning halfway around in the front seat.

"I don't know," answered Lindsey. "Tween twelve and fourteen, I guess." She turned to gaze out the car window. Everyone talked about wanting to be older. She wondered if they ever felt like she did, sometimes preferring to stay where she was. She didn't like changes. She had an ordinary life and she liked it. She liked her teacher, her little group of friends, her class in stained glass at the Y. Sometimes she even liked Jordan, the nerdy kid who lived across the street. Why grow up and go into the world when the world was a mess? Planes crashed and people starved and what could you do about it anyway?

"I wish I was fourteen," said Tosh. "Don't you

guys?" She leaned forward to turn up the volume on the radio.

"No, I don't really," replied Lindsey. Outside the window the unfamiliar streets, houses, and people were all zipping by. She felt a little strange herself and shook her head to try to clear it. "I wish I were a baked potato," she mumbled.

She *wished* right away that she could take it back. If she kept up this nonsense she'd end up going to the movies alone. She did the next best thing and started laughing.

"A baked potato?" said Lindsey's mom, who was driving. She began to laugh too, and then they all were. Lindsey suddenly felt relieved to be laughing, to get out of the throes of a junior high stress reaction caused by one simple assignment.

"What if I were a fried-egg sandwich?" cried Tosh. She laughed, slapping her thigh.

"I'm glad I'm not a cabbage. They look so stupid and naked and awful, like the head of a newborn baby!" Lorry slumped sideways, banging her head on the window.

"It's a fine source of vitamin C," said Anne, pulling into the parking lot. "Don't knock it."

Lindsey was glad they were laughing. They'd forgotton she was being kooky again.

"I know!" said Lorry, rubbing her head. "Let's change our names! I'm tired of the Snot Sisters. I'll be Tofu Pattie. Tosh, you can be Herb Peroshki! And . . ."

"And me?" asked Lindsey, leaning forward to hear.

"You?" Lorry turned, revealing a mean little smile. "You can be Nut Loaf."

The first person they saw at the mall asked them for money.

"I gave at the office," said Lorry, hurrying past the scruffy guy with his hand out.

"Lorry!" said Tosh.

"Hey, you can't save the world. C'mon, we're late."

"We *are* snots," said Lindsey, turning to glance at the guy, then running to catch up with her friends.

Once inside the mall she felt better. It was bright inside and full of pretty glitzy things. After the movie they wandered from store to store, but after a while she grew bored and restless. She didn't feel like trying on clothes, didn't feel like watching Lorry and Tosh try on clothes either.

She had a shoe in her hand when she heard that same gnattylike voice in her head. "Follow me," it beckoned. She cringed inside, put the shoe down, and ran off to find Tosh and Lorry, who were on their way to the fitting room armed with a load of swimsuits. She couldn't bear to sit through that. She'd meet them for ice cream in a half hour.

She wandered around for a while, then found herself flipping through cookbooks at B. Dalton. "You again," she muttered, gazing at photos of scalloped potatoes, onion-potato soup, and potato latkes drenched in sour cream and applesauce.

"I'm not writing about you," she mumbled. "Forget it. I don't know who you are or what you want, but I've got it all planned out. I'm writing about how I'm going to Jupiter to collect rocks and dirt and plants and how I'm going to study them under a microscope and live in an aluminum tent and talk to computers like Hal in the movie *2001*, and . . ."

The woman next to her was staring at her with a gaping mouth.

". . . now I've got to meet Tofu Pattie and Herb Peroshki for ice cream."

She had two scoops of Pralines 'n' Cream, her favorite.

On Monday morning Ms. Azumba stood in front of her desk with the unfinished essays in her hand. "Most of you are off to good starts. I've made some comments to help you along. Let's spend forty-five minutes more on these. Pass them back quickly. Don't waste time looking at your neighbor's paper."

Lindsey twirled a yellow pencil between her fingers as the papers were shuffled back down the rows. So far the worst had not happened. Ms. Azumba had not singled her out for a talk in private. Still, she did not look forward to reading her comments.

She took the paper from Andre and shut her eyes, then opened them one at a time. Perhaps Ms. Azumba had skipped her paper by mistake, but, no, there was a scrawl of blue ink across the bottom of the page. She quickly flattened her hand across it and first reread what she'd written on Friday.

"I'm glad I'm not a brown potato. If I were a brown

potato I'd be headed for trouble . . . potato potato potato. Brown brown brown brown brown shoe shoe desk desk this is a mess."

She flushed in embarrassment. How could she have written that? What did Ms. Azumba think of her now? Word by word, she slid her hand off Ms. Azumba's note.

"Trust your instincts. Go ahead with this original idea. . . ."

Startled, Lindsey lifted her hand, quickly reading the rest.

"What if you *were* a potato? What might it really be like?"

She reread Ms. Azumba's comments again and again. She was not kidding. She wanted her to write about being a potato. "What might it really be like?" She slapped the paper back down on the desk. How the heck should *I* know, she wondered. I was only *kidding*. I was *desperate* and the word popped into my mind out of nowhere. Now, how to get the darn thing to pop back out so that she could write about that space colony, get an *A*, and be done with it. "I'm not going to write about you. You're boring," she mumbled.

She realized by now, of course, that she'd begun to address the potato in a personal way. She was "commune-i-cating" with an inanimate object and considered ending her essay with this note to Ms. Azumba: "This is a danger-ous assignment."

Well, she had to get going. She picked up her pencil and wrote the title across the top of the paper. Then she drew in a deep breath and plunged in, but got to the middle of the first sentence and stopped. The next thought that was supposed to be there wasn't. She pulled at a piece of dead skin on her left little finger, feeling the onset of another junior high stress reaction. She told herself to calm down.

Lindsey glanced at the clock. About forty-one minutes to go. She gazed at the back of Andre's head, at the blue and white stripes in his collar, willing the next thought to come. She glared at the sheet of white paper for so long the desk and chair and the back of Andre's neck began to fade away. She felt lightheaded. She felt about to suffocate and grabbed the edge of her desk. She wanted to begin to describe the inside of her domed aluminum cabin on Jupiter but she couldn't see it. She smelled earth instead.

With the back of her left hand Lindsey felt her forehead. Maybe she was really ill, about to faint dead away. She closed her eyes, hoping it would happen. "What would it really be like?" was now a streak of blue ink and perspiration across her paper. She had to start writing. Forty minutes to go.

She put her pencil to the paper, took a deep breath, and began again, reminding herself it was only one assignment. "What if I were living . . ." she began. This time her hand jerked to a stop, and she felt a rush of tears to her eyes. It was no use. Something was terribly wrong. Wiping a few tears that had spilled onto her paper, a single phrase ran through her mind. "What might it really be like? What might it really be like? What might it really . . ." The white paper a window, a window . . . Her hand felt heavy, her head light. . . .

Lindsey rubbed her eyes and stretched her arms toward the ceiling. She was surprised to hear Ms. Azumba's familiar voice telling them to pass their papers forward because she felt as though she'd been away from the classroom. Looking down at what she'd written, she was shocked to see she'd filled three pages. No wonder her right hand ached.

All during lunch period Lindsey tried to evade Lorry's questions about her essay. "Why are you so interested in what I wrote?" she asked her.

"Because you won't tell me. That's why. What is that, salami? Trade you half a sandwich."

She had to evade her questions because she didn't remember. Curiously enough, she did not feel anxious. She felt relaxed and happy for the first time in days.

"You didn't say it had mustard on it," whined Lorry. "I don't like mustard."

"Picky picky. Scrape it off." She sipped from a carton of white milk, observing the dark scowl on Lorry's face, feeling a sudden urge to play Mrs. Potato Head. She mentally attached to Lorry's face a big red nose, two floppy pink ears, and a pair of horn-rimmed glasses.

"Why are you looking at me like that? Lindsey? *Lind-sey.* Earth to Bertha, Earth to Bertha."

"My friends call me Lumpy," said Lindsey.

Lorry rose slowly to her feet, scraping the legs of her

chair on the floor. "I'm worried about you, Lindsey," she said gravely. "You're changing and I don't like it."

By Wednesday, Ms. Azumba had graded the "es-SAYS." Once again they were passed, hand over shoulder, back down the rows of students. When Lindsey finally received hers she laid it flat on the desk and began to read.

Something to Say

I feel like something is about to happen. I hope so. I'm ready.

It is dark down here. The farther down you go the colder it gets so I stick close to the surface. Once in a while I go deeper because of the bugs but you can't stay down there. Not enough water. I am tired of the darkness, ready for light. I've never been up there but knowing gets passed down the vine. I know she is up there, and that's why I'm going.

Now I'm afraid. The ground has begun to shiver and I think I'll stay here after all. (These feelings are all mixed up with each other, like fine particles of sand and soil.) I guess I'm a coward. But what is that sound? I imagine it's my mama again, leaning over me whispering, passing on another story about our roots. It comes to me, through the water, through the earth, I don't know. I can feel a soft tingling coming down the shoots. Maybe it is the one about how we came up from the South, or back further to Ireland, to how we almost were wiped out by a fungus and a million people starved.

If I stay here something like that could happen to me.

What's going on? The soil around me is crumbling and I begin to tremble and shake. I'm so scared! So I elbow my way to the top to see what's going on. "Hey, yo, Skinhead, make way. Hey, Wormy, I'm coming up!"

It's crowded up near the top and I don't like it. But I carry my mama's words inside me. I can hear them whenever I want.

"There's a sweet potato patch close by," she says. "And a family of reds beyond that fence. They're all different, and they're all the same. They're all potatoes, fat ones and little skinny ones, big-eyed and small-eyed. There're mashers and hashers and fries. There're sweet potato pies. There are those that tell the truth and those that lie. . . ."

I stop listening to her and think about this whole family of potatoes spread all over this planet, potatoes, potatoes everywhere, all digging in and doing their work.

She can go on and on but I get her point. Like I am who I am and it's okay. To tell the truth, my friends call me Lumpy, I suppose for good reason. It's not much of a life compared to some, but it's a life, and I'm happy. I know where I'm going. So I smile at Skinhead here, and Wormy, just as my bed begins to shake again and a great noise nearly deafens me. Wait, I'm not really ready. Look at that spot on my middle. I can't go like that! Oh! A big warm thing around my middle, lifting me up . . . the light! The air! My eyes! Oh, Mama!

I'm falling, down to another dark place. Suddenly I'm up to my neck in other potatoes. There's Three-Eyes and

Baby. Say, Bob, say, Nancy, yo, Mudbutt. What a party! Here comes Earwig, watch out!

We are kept moving. Bags and crates, truck rides and storerooms. This has been an adventure!

Right now I'm nestled down here in the bottom of a bin, awaiting my turn. It'll come. Now that I've got this far, I understand.

The restaurant is empty and I am the last potato, bottom of the bin. The woman in the apron peers into the bin. "Hi, hon," she says. She winks, snatches me from the bin, scrubs me under a stream of running water. She knows. Into the microwave. Zap! I am about to burst with hope and pleasure. *She knows.* Now she wraps me in a manger of tinfoil. She carries me past the empty tables and chairs, out the front door into the wind, rain, and cold. There is a woman under a pile of rags in an alcove, a gray kitten curled on her lap. I pass from hand to hand. I see her face, oh, hope and glory. She eats.

It took quite some time to convince Tofu Pattie and Herb Peroshki to give up two hours a week. It was similar to baking a big Idaho potato long and slow in a regular oven instead of zapping it in a microwave. Change comes slowly.

But before the current year had ended, the Snot Sisters were washing and peeling potatoes every Wednesday afternoon at a soup kitchen not far from their school. Eventually they changed their name to the Spud Sisters and had new T-shirts made.

They all enjoyed the work and felt good about feeding the hungry. But nobody liked it as much as Lindsey. Sometimes, as she was bent low washing and peeling, washing and peeling, she could be heard whispering, "Hey, Bob, hey, Nancy, yo, Mudbutt. . . ."